THE RETURN OF THE DJINN

Borgo Press Books by BRIAN STABLEFORD

THE RETURN OF THE DJINN

AND OTHER BLACK MELODRAMAS

by

Brian Stableford

THE BORGO PRESS

An Imprint of Wildside Press LLC

MMIX

CONTENTS

INTRODUCTION

Comedy is black when it derives its humor from "the irony of fate," which dictates that "poetic justice" is intrinsically cruel: that moral order is never entirely conserved, always being subject to frictional losses, and often to frank inversion, subversion or perversion. It is the same with melodrama, although melodrama is generally expected to be intrinsically less vicious than comedy. Like comedy, melodrama is closely allied to horror, and generally benefits from a generous injection thereof, although the normal expectation in either case is that the horror component will eventually be balanced out—in the case of comedy by humorous deflation, and in the case of melodrama by climactic relief. Just as the punch-lines of black comedy are usually not very funny in hindsight, so the climaxes of black melodrama are usually rather disturbing when seen with the benefit of that same hindsight.

Writers of black melodrama often find it more comfortable to situate their stories in exotic settings, where the irony of fate has more elbow room to operate. The mythic past is a particularly useful locale, because it was custom-designed and serially refined by generations of storytellers to serve exactly that purpose; although "melodrama" is a modern category, it merely reproduces certain key features of the process that once routinely turned dimly-remembered events into the fabric of legend.

Although the quaintly misnamed gene of "science fiction" has done nothing to assuage the social leprosy forced on science by imbeciles incapable of getting intellectually to grips with it, it has provide a whole series of new settings that are easily adaptable to the purposes of black melodrama, including "secret histories" and "alternative histories". Other planets and the future (except for the very far future, when anything goes because everything recognizable can be safely assumed to have gone) are slightly less useful, because even science-phobic imbeciles know perfectly well that the mythic past has been dying since the day before its invention, and that its essential features become far less plausible when relocated from hypothetical pockets of the lost world to imaginary worlds based on the premise of their potential existence.

For this reason, the one science fiction story included in this collection—the first story—is set in the past rather than the future, dealing with an invention that somehow slipped out of the official record. On the other hand, "The Path of Progress" is not the only story here to deal with the possibility of progress; one of the richest sources of blackness in melodrama is the modern awareness that the people of the past—including the people of hypothetical pasts, including the multitudinous versions of the mythic past—could not see their own eras as we are now bound to see them: as stepping stones to our present.

The people of the past, like us, routinely saw their own world as one that was headed for hell in a hand-basket, having forsaken its former glories and raised a new generation of immoral slobs incapable of cherishing the glories of tradition. In modern accounts of past eras, therefore there is an inevitable dramatic tension between our notion of their innate dynamic and that possessed by the characters. This lends an extra dimension to "alternative mythical histories", which cannot help but embrace and embody alternative notions of progress and decay, and the potential contradictions between them. "Shadows of the Past" and, more particularly, "The Return of the Djinn", both attempt to trade in this admittedly-exotic narrative currency.

"Kalamada's Blessing" was originally published in *Scheherazade* 8 (1993) and "The Shepherd's Daughter" in the September 1990 issue of *Fear*; both stories were subsequently reprinted in a Necronomicon Press chapbook, *Fables and Fantasies* (1996). "Reconstruction" was initially published in *Cold Cuts II* (1994) edited by Paul Lewis and Steve Lockley. The other stories are original to this volume.

THE PATH OF PROGRESS

1.

The upper floors of the house overlooking Holland Park were almost completely dark, because the windows were shuttered in the continental style and all the shutters had been closed. Chinks of white gaslight showed through the wooden slats in one of the ground-floor rooms—Sir Julian Templeforth's study—and it was just possible to glimpse the ruddy glow of firelight in the master bedroom, which was doubtless being made comfortable in advance of the baronet's retirement. The unshuttered windows of the servants' quarters in the basement were, by contrast, all aglow with yellow candlelight; the staff still had two hours of the working day ahead of them.

Mathieu Galmier took off his hat before he rang the bell at the gate, acutely conscious of the fact that a Frenchman—even a former Professor of Medicine at the Sorbonne—was expected to be humble in this part of London, even before lackeys who were not, strictly speaking, English themselves. It was a long time since Britain and France had last been formally at war, but no one in the British Isles had forgotten Waterloo, and those who read the newspapers knew that any vestiges of French dignity that had survived Bonaparte's fall had been shattered and ground into the dust at Sedan, less than twenty years ago.

The concierge, Reilly—who preferred to be called a porter—scowled at Mathieu as he opened the gate, and did not trouble to accompany him to the perron, to which Sir Julian always referred as "the front steps". Cormack, the butler who answered the door in response to the second bell, was too haughty to scowl, but that did not mean that he looked upon his master's guest with any conspicuous approval. Cormack was duty-bound to accompany Mathieu to the study door and introduce him, once he had collected the visitor's rain-soaked coat and hat, but he was not required to purge his conscientiously-schooled voice of all disdain, and he took full advantage of that license.

Sir Julian was endeavoring to relax in a leather-upholstered armchair with a glass of brandy and a volume from Mudie's library, but he gave the impression of having a great deal on his mind. He made no show of being glad to see his visitor, but he got to his feet, smoothed the creases in his blood-red waistcoat and adjusted the ruffed sleeves of his old-fashioned shirt.

"Come in, Professor," Sir Julian said, suppressing a sigh and inviting Mathieu with a casual gesture to take his armchair's twin, positioned on the other side of the fireplace. "Is there a problem with regard to tomorrow's appointment?"

Mathieu sat down. He declined the glass of brandy that Sir Julian offered him by means of another quasi-theatrical gesture. The baronet waved Cormack away; the butler closed the study door behind him, ostentatiously clicking the catch to emphasize that his master's privacy was guaranteed.

"There *is* a problem, Sir Julian," Mathieu said, bluntly. "As I warned you at the time, I was unable to retain enough of the agent following the last administration to continue the principal course of the experimental scheme. Given the desperate need to find a means of reproducing the agent, if the project is not to reach an impasse...."

"What you mean," Sir Julian said, cutting him off, "is that you want me to bring you more money tomorrow."

"I do need more money, Sir Julian," Mathieu said, tiredly, relaxing into the comfortable leather upholstery in spite of his anxiety and determination to remain alert, "but I also need more...volunteers. If you continue to increase your personal demand for the agent—and I'm not denying your need for larger and more frequent doses—then the supply has to be increased commensurately. It's as much in your interest as mine that I find a means of producing the agent *in vitro*. I told you when we began this project that I could not put a firm price on the achievement, nor specify a time-limit. Organic chemistry is in its infancy, as is microbiology. We're explorers and pioneers, attempting to beat the path of progress on a trackless frontier."

"Don't talk like some damned American," Sir Julian observed. "You're a man of science, not an Indian scout. You were supposed to be Pasteur's most promising pupil—the man to take medical biology into a new era. Perhaps I should have befriended the one with the Russian name and left you to the mercy of the gendarmerie. It's all very well for you to talk about needing an increased supply, more money and more time—we all need time, and my need is the most pressing of all. Your job is to deliver it, not to demand it. I don't understand this obsession with inducing the so-called agent to reproduce. The original idea was simply to extract it and employ it as a vaccine, like Jenner's. It wasn't supposed to require more than one dose, let alone doses of increasing magnitude and frequency. I understand that explorers don't always find what they're hoping to find, but when they don't, they have to tailor their plans to what they do find. Cormack can get you more raw material easily enough, I suppose, but there are risks, as you know only too well."

"The risks will be a thing of the past," Mathieu told him, "if and when I can find a substrate that will enable me to maintain and reproduce the agent outside the human body. If that can be done, we won't need any more…raw material."

"*If and when,*" Sir Julian repeated, thumping the am of his chair with a closed fist. "It's always *if and when* with you, Monsieur Galmier. Well, girls are cheap enough, and there's no shortage of supply, but you're already costing me too dear in rent, laboratory equipment and living expenses. There's a limit to the indulgence you can expect in terms of buying new equipment and messing about with *substrates.*"

Sir Julian was staring at Mathieu in a markedly insistent fashion, as if he were attempting to mesmerize his visitor, or at least to dominate him by the power of his will. The stare was difficult to resist, even though it had no occult force. Mathieu had to admit though, that the baronet had the appearance of an idealized natural aristocrat, possessed of an innate right to rule. Sir Julian's actual title was meager, but his bearing was not; he gave the impression of being a seventeenth-century Cavalier displaced into the nineteenth century by some freak of time, reminiscent of a lush Dutch portrait of Prince Rupert of the Rhine.

Sir Julian Templeforth was an exceptionally handsome man nowadays, Mathieu thought, proudly. There was nothing in the least unmasculine about him—indeed, he had an exceptionally robust and virile frame—but his face had a particular perfection of form and complexion that was rarely seen in a male of the species. His black hair was sleek and glossy, with a hint of a natural curl, and his sky-blue eyes had a clarity that was quite marvelous, even in the Celtic type that routinely combined dark hair with blue or green eyes. If ever there was an irresistible stare, Mathieu thought, this was it—but he had to resist it, if he could. Given that it was, in a sense, his invention, he ought to be able to do it.

"The extraction process runs much more smoothly now that I've mastered it," the scientist persisted, patiently. "I've also improved the filtration process and acquired considerable skill in the purification of the agent, but I need to take the next step. Even if we were to set other considerations aside, and regard the project as a merely personal matter, we can't be content to continue doing extractions at increasingly frequent intervals. Eventually, something will go wrong, in spite of all my precautions. Many of these girls are carrying multiple infections, none of which we fully understand. So far, in my opinion, you've been exceptionally lucky. I've been keeping close track of Elie Metchnikoff's immunological work at the Institut, as well as Monsieur Pasteur's quest for new vaccines and the latest advances in apochromatic microscopy. Everything suggests that the range of pathogenic agents is much greater than was first supposed. If I can't isolate the agent in which we're interested, and discover out how to reproduce it *in vitro,* there's a risk that you might lose everything I've so far been able to do for you."

Sir Julian got to his feet, perhaps hoping to increase the dominating effect of his stare, but after looking down at his visitor for a few seconds he turned away. His eyes went to the portrait hanging over the fireplace: the portrait of his father, who had fought at Waterloo as a mere subaltern and had subsequently commanded a brigade in the Crimea, where he had somehow avoided being singled out by *The Times* as yet another glaring exemplar of British military incompetence. Sir Malcolm Templeforth had not been a handsome man, and his son—who looked far too young to be the older man's child—did not resemble him at all.

"Things are bad in Ireland and getting worse," Sir Julian said, suppressing another sigh. "Ever since Gladstone gave the rebels that first inch they've been determined to take far more than a mile. Even with an honest steward in place, the estate's revenues are sinking like a stone. The poor fellow's under siege. Even bog-Irish peasants are taught to read nowadays, it seems, and encouraged to delude themselves that they're capable of philosophical thought. What they read, alas, is the radical press, and the form their philosophy takes is obsession with the rights of man, trades unions and all that nonsense. My tenants have formed some sort of association, it seems, and badger my steward daily with lists of grievances. He's demanding, on their behalf, that I go over there—not requesting, you understand, but *demanding*. He won't believe me when I say that I can't, although you know full well that I really can't leave London now. It wouldn't do any good, of course, if I did go—the wretches complain bitterly about absentee landlords, but they make it impossible for anyone to work comfortably in residence."

Mathieu did not know how to respond to this tirade, and began to wish that he had accepted the offer of a brandy, if only to have something to do with his hands.

"Anyway," Sir Julian went on, "my purse isn't bottomless, and I'm feeling the pinch at present. There's no way I can increase my funds, except perhaps by marrying again, but the marriage market isn't what it was thirty years ago. I could probably snag some damned American whose father's in steel or oil, although they all seem to want an earldom at least, but that would take time." He paused before adding: "You're not thinking about looking for another backer, are you? You do realize how unwise that would be?"

The way the questions were phrased made them appear to be defensive moves in the face of a hypothetical threat, but Mathieu knew that they constituted a serious threat in themselves, and perhaps a deadly one. He had always known that Sir Julian was a dangerous man. At first, he had obtained a certain thrill from playing with fire—but he was older now, and the ultimate objective of his research seemed to be as far away as ever, in spite of all his efforts. Had he been prepared to serve as his own subject, he thought, his history might have been quite different. Unlike Sir Julian, though, he had never been reckless, rich or lucky.

"I'm fully aware of the trouble you could cause for me," Mathieu observed, quietly, "and the violence you might do to me. I sometimes wonder whether I might have been thrown to the wolves already, or worse, had the agent been as successful as we first hoped."

"And I sometimes wonder whether you might be playing me like a fish," Sir Julian retorted, "keeping me hooked by deliberately doling out your drug in doses that become less effective by degrees, simply in order to keep extracting money for me to fund your greater ambitions. But we mustn't let such suspicions get the better of us. We trusted one another once—it would be better for both of us if we still did."

That was true, but Mathieu was saved from having to admit it by a discreet knock on the door.

Cormack waited for his master to call out a summons before he opened it, and came in hesitantly. "I'm very sorry to disturb you sir," the butler said, "but I thought you ought to know that there is someone watching the house from the bushes in Holland Park. According to Reilly, he took up his post immediately after Mr. Galmier's arrival, and might perhaps have been following him."

Sir Julian fixed Mathieu with a different kind of stare, which testified eloquently to the extent of the loss of trust between them.

"I had no idea!" Mathieu protested. "I wouldn't have been able to take a hansom, even if I'd tried, because of the rain…."

"That wouldn't have made a damn bit of difference, you fool," Sir Julian said, hotly. "The point is, who is he? And how did you attract his attention in the first place?"

Mathieu shook his head, helplessly.

Sir Julian was not a man to waste time in circumstances like these. He went to the cabinet beside the door and took out his father's old saber, with a promptitude that suggested to Mathieu that he always relished an opportunity to do so. Rumor had it that he had killed half a dozen men in duels—though none, as yet, on English soil.

"Tell Reilly to work his way around behind the fellow if he can," the baronet instructed Cormack. "He'll need a stout cudgel, but tell him not to wield it too brutally. We want to question the man, not split his skull. We'll leave five minutes, then we'll come out of the front door and make directly for the spy."

Cormack nodded, and hurried away to relay the order. Sir Julian raised the saber and weighed it in his hand, in eager anticipation.

"The fellow can't see anything, with all the shutters closed," Mathieu pointed out. "His vigil will be wasted."

"Even if he didn't follow you here," Sir Julian said, "he'll probably follow you home, given the chance. The mere fact that he's aware of our association means that he knows too much—enough, at any rate, for us to need to know exactly how much he does know, and what his interest is." The baronet put on his black coat, donning a kind of emphatic arrogance with it that Mathieu could not help but think of as Rocambolesque, although Sir Julian would probably have preferred "Wellingtonian". Cormack had brought Mathieu's coat too, which was shabbier by far.

When the five minutes had elapsed, Sir Julian made for the main door of the house, beckoning to Mathieu as if he were commanding a footman. Mathieu followed, content to remain three paces in rear.

Sir Julian bounded down the steps and raced through the open gate, crossing the deserted street in three strides—but there were iron railings around the park, and the nearest gate was ten yards to one side, requiring an awkward detour. As Sir Julian headed for the gate there was a flurry of movement in the bushes beyond the railings, and the quarry set off like a startled hare.

Reilly, alas, was no greyhound. By the time Sir Julian had reached the place where the watcher had been stationed, the porter had already engaged the spy in a brief scuffle, but had been knocked down without being able to bring his cudgel into play. By the time Mathieu caught up with his patron, the baronet was fulminating at his aged retainer. Reilly complained in vain that the unknown man had been considerably taller, younger and stronger than he was, and that the grass had been exceedingly slippery after the rain.

Sir Julian rounded on Mathieu then. "This is your fault," he declared, although Mathieu knew that no one had any real reason to suppose that it was. "Make sure that no one follows you home, if you can. I'll come tomorrow, at seven, as arranged. You'll have the usual delivery before noon, but I'll try to make provision for another before the end of the week. I'll bring some extra money for you—but I warn you that I expect results. You'd better find a means to grow the vaccine in a flask pretty damned quick, else you and I will need a further reckoning."

"This kind of adventurous research can't be done to order," Mathieu said, feeling obliged to mount some kind of formal protest. "There's no precedent to guide us."

"Necessity," Sir Julian stated, with not a hint of irony, "is the mother of improvisation. It was you who put yourself under its spur—where I've long grown used to living. There's no use complaining that you need more time when the sand has all but run through the hour-glass. If that was a policeman, he's more likely to be after you than me—which means that you need me even more than I need you, and not just for money. Whether you walk back to your lodgings or take a cab, *keep looking behind you*."

2.

Cormack brought the girl in person, arriving shortly before noon, as promised. She was no more than thirteen, in Mathieu's judgment, although she claimed when asked to be sixteen. Either way, she seemed unlikely to reach twenty, whatever was done or not done to her in the meantime. She told Mathieu that her name was Judy Lee, which he had no reason to doubt.

"Do you know why you're here, Judy?" Mathieu asked, when Cormack had gone, leaving him alone with the girl in his laboratory, which was constructed in the only large room in his basement flat south of Goldhawk Road.

"Y'r gwin t'bleed me," the girl said. "Bin cupped afore—din' do me no good, though they said it would." She looked around anxiously, intimidated by the mass of apparatus. She had surely never been to a public lecture at the Royal Institution, so the only place she might have seen such an assembly of equipment before was on the stage of some cheap theatre. Laboratory equipment had been the standard décor of exaggerated melodrama ever since Mary Shelley's *Frankenstein* has been adapted for the Porte-Saint-Martin more than sixty years before.

"I'm not going to cup you," Mathieu said, as soothingly as he could. "I'm going to insert two hollow needles into veins in your forearms. I'll swab the flesh with alcohol first to sterilize it. The cooling effect of the alcohol's evaporation will help numb the pain. I'm going to leave the needles in place for some time, so that I can put the blood I draw from one vein through a special filter, and then return it to the other. It might seem rather horrid, but it's quite safe. One day, in the not-too-distant future, it will be standard practice in hospitals all over the world."

"I had worse done to me," Judy Lee reported, making an effort to remain laconic. Mathieu had no reason to doubt that, either. He thought it best to keep talking, not so much by way of paying lip-service to the principle of informed consent as to reassure her that this was something that he had done before, many times, and that it really would become a normal aspect of medical practice—*scientific* medical practice, not quackery or the obsolete traditions that the majority of physicians still insisted on following.

"You're contributing to an important study, Judy," he assured her. "You and I are adventurers on the path of progress."

The girl attempted to smile, but she had not been a whore long enough to have mastered that kind of insincerity. She was still beautiful, as much because of the consumption that had begun to eat her away as in spite of it. The disease gave a certain semi-transparent gloss to the skin and sculpted her lean features, exaggerating the eyes in a strangely soulful fashion. He told himself that she would not be beautiful much longer, whether he intervened in the process of her deterioration or not, and that it might be good for her to be saved from a career of prostitution, if that turned out to be the result of her participation in his project.

One day, Mathieu thought, he would be able to pay back what he took from his "volunteers", with abundant interest. Soon enough, if he were only allowed time and adequate financial support, he would find a way to isolate the bacillus—or whatever term he might invent to substitute for "bacillus"—and feed it *in vitro*, so that it would be able reproduce itself independently of its host. Then the transactions in which he dealt would no longer be a matter of robbing Petronella to pay Paul, but a matter of assisting in the evolution of humankind, of building a hitherto-unimaginable Utopia on the rickety foundations of London's slums.

"French, aintcher?" the girl said, as the second needle went in. The original syringe, having injected the anti-clotting serum, had been hooked up to the pump and the filtration apparatus. Now Mathieu hooked up the second modified syringe, completing the circuit. He had good grounds, now, to be sure that he could feed at least three liters of the girl's blood through the machine without undue risk, although he would have to give her careful instructions to limit subsequent blood-loss, given that the anti-clotting agent would remain in her bloodstream for anything up to three days. It had been the induced hemophilia that had caused two of the three fatal casualties in Paris, rather than the extraction process itself, but a Parisian tribunal would have been unlikely to appreciate the nice distinction. There had only been one fatal accident since he had decamped to London—but that would likely prove to be one too many, if the spy who had been watching Sir Julian's house the night before really had been a policeman investigating his activities.

"That's right," Mathieu admitted, without looking up from his work. "I worked with Louis Pasteur before I came to London."

"Heard o' him," Judy Lee boasted. "Germs 'n' that."

"That's right," Mathieu said, approvingly. "He's developed a method of sterilizing milk too, and a treatment for rabies. A great man—a very great man. The Institut is also doing experiments in blood transfusion, now that the legal prohibition has been lifted. We lost two hundred years of potential progress in that regard, because the scientific method came into conflict with the law. The first blood transfusions were carried out within walking distance of this very spot, by Sir Christopher Wren—the man who designed Saint Paul's Cathedral—in 1657. He was hoping to find a method of rejuvenation, but it turned out that one man's blood is sometimes another man's poison. My countryman, Jean-Baptiste Denis, was sued by the widow of a man who died in the course of one of his transfusion experiments, and the practice was outlawed.

"All that was necessary was to figure out a simple pattern of incompatibilities—even the primitive microscopes of the day would have been adequate to the necessary investigations—but the work wasn't done because no one dared take the risk of prosecution. If they'd persisted, all kinds of surgery would have become safer and more effective two hundred years ago—the metalworkers of the day would have been easily able to produce hollow needles and Pravaz syringes, if only there had been a manifest need for them. As things turned out, though, it took another two hundred years to put together the kind of apparatus that could replace blood lost in surgery, just as I'm now replacing yours.

"Scientific medicine might have made vast strides in the eighteenth century, if only medical scientists had been permitted to experiment. Instead, there was a Golden Age of quackery, when all kinds of bizarre patent medicines flourished, while orthodox physicians fought tooth and nail to defend their own superstitions. The possible deaths of a few dozen or a few hundred volunteers in controlled experiments were prevented, while hundreds of thousands of people who had no choice at all died by virtue of licensed but misguided treatments, and millions more by virtue of ignorant inaction. Things are different now—very different—but the necessary research requires time, and money, which is direly hard to come by. If the governments of Europe would only take their responsibilities seriously, instead of spending all their time and revenues plotting and preparing for war, there'd be no need for self-serving buccaneers like Sir Julian Temp...."

He trailed off, realizing that his tongue had run away with him, and that it was perhaps as well that the girl could not be expected to understand what he was saying. "I'm sorry," he said. "What I mean is that you're helping in a great cause, and have every reason to be proud of yourself."

"Doin' it for the money," she observed, dully. "Y'c'n buy a girl in Bethnal Green for a shilling—a guinea's good scratch. Done worse for far less."

Mathieu gritted his teeth. "One day," he said, in a low voice, "my work will do wonders for girls like you. You'll be its true beneficiaries, at the end of the day. The twentieth century will be a new Age of Miracles, not just for the rich but for everyone. Do you mind if I leave you now, just for a little while? I'll come back in ten or fifteen minutes."

Judy Lee nodded. Mathieu knew that he really ought to stay, but her taciturnity was putting undue stress on his conversational skills, and the atmosphere in the subterranean laboratory was becoming foul with the reek of blood. He needed fresh air—and today, fortunately, was one of the rare days on which London's air really was fresh. Yesterday's rain had washed the accumulated smog-particles out of the atmosphere, and a brisk south-westerly breeze was preventing its reformation. Although the new network of sewers had not yet taken up the entirety of the river's burden, the days of the Great Stink were long gone.

Mathieu went up the steps to the pavement of the street and leaned against the railings protecting the hollow in which his front door was set. There was a faint unsteady vibration beneath his feet, which was primarily a side-effect of the construction-work on the underground railway, although the excavation of the sewers still had a minor contribution to make. London's Underworld was a complex hive of activity now, with countless workers toiling round the clock in shifts, largely unnoticed by the denizens of the surface.

Men of science, Mathieu thought, were not unlike those subterranean laborers, their patiently heroic endeavors being largely unheeded by journalists and historians alike. The chroniclers of the modern world, like the chroniclers of the Middle Ages, paid close attention to the actions of kings, statesmen and generals, but rarely noticed the subtle revolutions in technology that were the true motor of history.

Mathieu realized, however, that he was not presently unobserved. There was a tall, lean man bundled up in a dark blue overcoat leaning casually on the railings of the house opposite, who never looked at him directly but never excluded him from his field of vision either. Mathieu had no idea whether it was the same man who had been watching Sir Julian's house the previous evening, and had no way of determining whether or not the watcher might be a police detective, but he was in no doubt that he and his lodgings were under surveillance. The laboratory was invisible from the street, and from the back yard too—the apartment's only front window looked into Mathieu's kitchen, while the rear window was in his tiny bedroom—but that did not make him feel any more comfortable.

He went back inside immediately, and hurried back to the girl, who was drowsy but seemed as well as could possibly be expected. He fed her a small measure of port wine, holding the glass to her lips so that she did not have to move her arms. When he had detached the needles and bandaged the residual wounds he gave her a generous cup of hot sweet tea and a slice of toast with marmalade before sending her on her way. She was a little unsteady on her feet but she could walk perfectly well. She looked around as he ushered her through the hallway, taking what note she could of the circumstances of his life.

"I c'n come back, if y'like" she said, as he opened the door. "For company, mind, not blood." She sounded genuinely hopeful, perhaps because he seemed a cut above her usual clients, or merely because she thought him a likely prospect.

"No," he said, brusquely. "Please don't come here again—not ever." He knew that she probably would, when the after-effects set in, but he had learned to steel himself against such occasions, and to turn the visitors away.

The watcher on the other side of the street did not budge from his station when Mathieu escorted the girl back up to the pavement, and did not follow her when she made her way back to Goldhawk Road. He studied the girl as she walked away, though, before returning his eyes to Mathieu's lodgings, abruptly enough to catch Mathieu's gaze for a moment. Mathieu judged, as the two of them locked stares momentarily, that the other man knew perfectly well that he had been spotted, but did not care. The watcher's eyes were dark and keen. His short-cropped hair gave him the appearance of a seaman, and the uneven coloring of his face suggested that he had recently shaved off a well-grown beard and moustache.

Mathieu hurried back to his laboratory, to begin work on the filtrate; it was a few minutes after four o'clock, and he was anxious to get the preparatory work done before Sir Julian arrived. He wanted the laboratory to be spick and span, to present an image of efficient, dedicated and productive labor. He wanted Sir Julian to feel confident that his money was being well spent, and would prove to be an excellent investment, on his own behalf and the world's.

Mathieu tried to put Judy Lee's image out of his mind. He did not want to see her again, under any circumstances. By the time her blood was clotting properly again—if she suffered no serious mishap before then—the change would be becoming noticeable. Within a week, at the most, the metamorphosis would be complete. Time would ameliorate the problem slightly, as the indwelling population of the agent began to increase again, but experience suggested that it would never be able to make up the deficit that his filtration had caused. All the evidence he had so far collected suggested that she would never recover what she had lost.

Mathieu split the filtrate into two unequal, parts: one for Sir Julian and one for the continuation of his *in vitro* experiments. He would dearly have loved to retain the larger fraction for the latter purpose, but he did not dare. Sir Julian's need—if need were the right word—was increasing too rapidly. Had the baronet been given the choice, Mathieu would probably have been instructed to reserve all the filtrate for his use, but Mathieu still had power enough within their relationship to insist that the broader purpose be maintained. Sir Julian had had plenty of opportunity to see what happened to the "volunteers" who provided him with the means to maintain his condition, and he knew exactly how valuable Mathieu's expertise was. As a last resort, the baronet might take the chance of replacing him with some ambitious graduate of Guy's or St Thomas's—but only as a last resort. Theirs was the kind of Faustian bargain that could not easily be substituted, on either side.

3.

While Mathieu was working on the filtrate, the oil-lamps illuminating the laboratory began to burn low. One of them went out, but it was the more distant of the two from his work-bench and he did not immediately get up to refill it. His supply of oil was running low, and it would be better to make do with one lamp, if he could, at least until Sir Julian had handed over the promised cash. His work would have been more brightly served by gaslight, of course, but the laboratory was only fitted with a single gas tap, which he reserved for his Bunsen burner.

Had Mathieu's rooms been located under the eaves of the house, instead of in the basement, he would have been able to work by daylight, but when he and Sir Julian had selected his place of work they had both thought a windowless room best suited to their purpose. At that time, they really had imagined that a single dose of the "vaccine" might suffice to work a miracle that could be repeated a hundred times over, but the combination of Jenner's practice and Pasteur's theory had not been as simple as Mathieu had hoped. The fundamental thesis had been sound enough—it really did seem to be the case that Jenner's vaccine worked because it transmitted a biological agent of some kind, rather than by observance of some strange homeopathic principle—but it had proved impossible to construct a strictly analogical procedure with respect to the agent that Mathieu's fungal filters had caught. The human microcosm was, it seemed, even more complicated than the macrocosm that scientific astronomy had recently begun to reveal, with the aid of photography, spectroscopes and increasingly powerful lenses.

When Mathieu heard the click of a catch in the corridor outside the laboratory he immediately looked up at the clock, which indicated half past six. Sir Julian had a key to the front door, of course, and was not given to ringing doorbells, but he was a punctual man and it was unlike him to be early, even when he was anxious.

Mathieu looked around for something that might serve as a weapon, and picked up a scalpel from the bench. He moved to the door, but did not reach for the knob; instead, he positioned himself so that he would be concealed behind it if it were opened.

It did open, very quietly, and swung inwards slowly. That, too, was not Sir Julian's way—he was a man more inclined to throw doors open and march in boldly, no matter what the circumstances of his arrival might be. Whoever was opening the door now was peering in gingerly, attempting to look around before setting foot across the threshold. Had the intruder been anyone with a legitimate reason for being there, he would surely have called out, but he seemed intent on maintaining the strictest silence.

Mathieu did not wait for the invader to step inside, but put his shoulder to the door while the other was still within the compass of its swing, and shoved it with all his might. The other, quite unprepared for such an assault, cursed loudly and yielded ground—but did not fall over and immediately began to shove back.

It was obvious to Mathieu that his adversary was the stronger man, for he felt himself gradually pressed back against the wall, trapped by the pressure of the solid wooden door. He reached round the batten and slashed downwards with the scalpel. The thrust brought forth another curse, but the blade had caught the sleeve of a thick overcoat, and it was not a wounding blow. The other leaned on the door even harder, trying to crush the breath from Mathieu's body.

Mathieu cried out for help, although he had no reason at all to think that any might be close at hand. The crushing pressure continued, and he shouted again, knowing that he might not have enough breath left for a third appeal. He lashed out with the scalpel twice more, but now that his assailant knew that the instrument was in his hand, the thrusts cleaved empty air.

Mathieu knew that he was beaten, and had just decided to issue his surrender and beg for mercy when the weight pressing on the door was suddenly relieved. There was the noise of a sudden furious tussle on the other side of it, and then the sound of running feet as one of the two combatants—presumably the one who had been using the door to crush him—scrambled for the front door.

Mathieu moved around the door ready to greet his rescuer, assuming that he would see Sir Julian—but the man standing in the corridor watching his erstwhile opponent beat an ungainly retreat was the man who had been leaning on the railings opposite, watching the house. For a moment, Mathieu assumed that the wrong combatant had been bested, and raised the hand clutching the scalpel as if to stab is enemy—but then he realized that the watcher really had run to rescue him, and that the man who was now running up the steps beyond the front door was completely unknown to him. It seemed that Mathieu really had had a narrow escape, because the man who was running away was every bit as tall, and even more heavily-built, than the man who had come to his aid.

Mathieu hesitated over what to do next—and while he hesitated, the watcher from the far side of the street grabbed his wrist and disarmed him, saying: "No need for that, Frenchy." His accent had a distinct cockney twang, but that was no guarantee that he was not a policeman. At close range, Mathieu was able to estimate that the darker parts of the man's complexion were the consequence of exposure to tropical sunlight. The dark blue overcoat was, in fact, the sort worn by merchant seamen, and his heavily-callused hands provided that final proof that he was indeed a sailor recently returned from a long voyage.

"Who are you?" Mathieu finally found the courage to demand.

"A friend, it seems—at least for the moment."

"Why were you watching my house? Have you been following me?"

"As a matter of fact," the tall man said "I started off following the fellow who brought the girl."

While this terse conversation was taking place, the newcomer's gaze had made a careful tour of the gloomy laboratory. His dark eyes did not give much away, but Mathieu judged that he had not had the slightest expectation of seeing this kind of apparatus, and was now wondering what kind of alchemist's den he had stumbled into.

"Why?" Mathieu asked, bluntly.

"Because I was told in Stepney that he once collected another girl in exactly the same fashion—one who hasn't been seen since by her mother, sister or aunt."

Mathieu's heart sank. *Not the police, then*, he thought. *At least not yet—but trouble all the same. On the other hand, he can't be certain that the other girl was also brought here.* "What do you want with me?" he asked, aloud.

"That I don't quite know, as yet," the stranger replied. "What did *he* want with you, do you think?" He nodded towards the door through which the other invader had made his escape, which still stood open.

"A common sneak-thief, I suppose," Mathieu said, wishing that he sounded more convincing.

"This place reeks of blood," the tall man observed. "What in God's name are you doing here?"

"Medical research," Mathieu retorted, taking slight offense at the other's tone. "Work for the benefit and progress of humankind."

Perhaps remarkably, given that he seemed no better educated than the young whore, the stranger did not seem disinclined to take that statement at face value. "What kind of…?" he began, not unrespectfully.

The seaman did not have time to complete the sentence before a new voice cut in, saying: "I do not think, sir, that the professor's work is any concern of yours."

Mathieu and the stranger both turned to the open doorway, where Sir Julian Templeforth was now standing. The briefest sideways glance at the clock told Mathieu that the baronet was as punctual as ever.

The stranger looked the baronet up and down, and lowered his eyes reflexively in the face of that brilliant blue-eyed stare.

"Who is this, Mathieu?" Sir Julian demanded, with a note of accusation in his voice.

"I don't know his name, sir," Mathieu was quick to say, "but he came to my aid when I called for help just now, and frightened off a man who was attacking me—a burglar, I suppose, who must have thought the dwelling empty, having seen no light from the front."

"I'm Thomas Dean, merchant seaman," the tall man supplied, promptly, "lately second mate on the SS *Hallowmas*."

Thomas Dean waited politely, but Sir Julian did not introduce himself. Instead, he reached into his jacket pocket for his pocketbook, saying: "We're grateful for your help. Perhaps...."

"I don't want your money," the seaman interrupted, his voice turning harsh. "I want to know what's going on here. I want to know what that girl was doing here this afternoon, and whether the same thing that was done to her, whatever it might be, was also done to my sister Caroline."

Sir Julian's eyes narrowed, and his hand fell away from his jacket pocket towards his britches, where there was a very conspicuous bulge. If Sir Julian wanted to carry a revolver, Mathieu thought, he might do better to wear looser-fitting trousers with more capacious pockets—like the ones the sailor had on. He found, somewhat to his alarm, that he could not remember Caroline Dean at all. He was at least fifty per cent sure, though, that the girl who had died—the only one, so far as he knew, to have died since he came to London—had had a different name.

"Mr. Dean followed a man who brought a young girl here this afternoon," Mathieu said, trying to let his patron know, without giving the game away, that the seaman did not appear to be aware of the connection between Cormack and Sir Julian. He made a private observation that the lack of any such awareness made it unlikely that Thomas Dean had been the man who was watching the house in Holland Park on the previous night, before adding: "He thinks the same man might have taken his sister away. If so, Mr. Dean, he did not bring her here. He probably supplies girls to more than one client."

Dean's gaze went from Mathieu to Sir Julian and back again, then made another thoughtful tour of the laboratory. He made no attempt to hide his suspicions. "In that case," he said, "I'd best take what I know to Scotland Yard, and let the police...."

The seaman broke off as Sir Julian produced the revolver from his pocket, but a slight smile flashed across his lips. Mathieu inferred that Dean's suspicions had just been turned into certainty. As an officer on an ocean-going vessel he was presumably required to carry a gun himself on occasion, and he did not seem to be in the least intimidated by the weapon. Mathieu, on the other hand, knew that Sir Julian was as expert with a pistol as he was with a blade, and was certainly reckless enough to make use of his expertise if the impulse came upon him. The baronet had obviously leapt to the conclusion that Caroline Dean *had* been the girl who had died, even though he had a poorer memory for names of that sort than Mathieu.

Sir Julian closed the door behind him and turned the key in the lock. "You should have taken the money, lad," he said, softly. "By the look of you, I doubt that your blood has anything to contribute to the professor's research, but a man of science can always find a use for such stuff, if it comes to that. If you behave yourself, though, we'll settle for tying you up and putting you to bed in the professor's cupboard for a little while."

Mathieu groaned audibly, knowing that the situation was now beyond all possibility of control. "What about the other one?" he murmured. "What if *he* turns out to be the one who was watching us in Holland Park?"

Sir Julian evidently had not considered that possibility. After a moment's pause, though, he shrugged his shoulders. "We can't stay here now, in any case," he said. "It looks as if we'd best be Ireland-bound, no matter how much trouble the goddam rebels are causing over there. We'll have to go ahead with tonight's treatment, as planned, but then we must start packing up. Do you have some rope with which to tie the fellow up?"

"Only twine," Mathieu said, looking towards the shelf that accommodated a stout ball of sturdy string.

"Best do a good job, then," Sir Julian said. "He's a sailor, after all, well used to dealing with knots. If he gets loose, I'll have to shoot him—and that's not what any of us wants." This statement was, of course, intended to impress the logic of the situation upon Dean rather than Mathieu, but Mathieu could see, as he reached for the ball of string, that the seaman had made his own estimate of that logic.

Mathieu had quite forgotten the scalpel, and Sir Julian evidently had not noticed that Thomas Dean was carrying anything. The instrument was, after all, quite small and the seaman's hand was larger than average. Mathieu's blood ran suddenly cold as the sailor suddenly flipped his wrist and sent the scalpel hurtling towards Sir Julian's face. The baronet saw it coming too late, and probably had no idea what it was until the object struck him full in the face. The sharp blade sliced into the cheek, about an inch below his right eye, and cut through the flesh until its progress was arrested by the cheekbone.

Sir Julian howled, more in wrath than in pain, and jerked his head to one side.

The wound bled copiously, but Mathieu could not imagine that it was serious. The blade fell to the floor, but Sir Julian had closed his eyes reflexively even as he raised the pistol in order to take aim. Before the baronet could open his eyes again, in order to complete the threatening gesture, Dean had grabbed Mathieu and pulled him into position as a human shield. Dean's left arm was now around Mathieu's neck, while the right held a much larger knife, with a curved blade and a serrated edge, which he must have had concealed about his person.

While Mathieu felt the point of Dean's knife digging suggestively into his neck, not far from the carotid artery, Sir Julian tried to stem the blood coursing from his cheek with his left hand, while holding the revolver as steadily as he could in his right. Eventually, the baronet fished a handkerchief from his pocket and pressed it to the wound. The white cotton turned red, but the further flow of blood was inhibited. The baronet's eyes were livid with anger, but he was in control of himself and his right hand was not trembling.

"Now," said Dean, a trifle hoarsely, "let's take stock. It seems that the man I put to flight might not have been a common-or-garden burglar after all—in which case, he might come back. On the whole, though, we're not likely to be disturbed, at least for a little while. Time to complete the introductions, I think. Who are you?"

"Go to hell," Sir Julian said. If Mathieu could read the sky-blue eyes correctly, Sir Julian was weighing up the possibility of taking a shot anyway, carefully weighing up his chances of hitting the seamen in the head without Mathieu ending up with a cut throat.

"I'm Mathieu Galmier, late of the Sorbonne and the Institut Pasteur," Mathieu was quick to say. "I'm doing research in immunology, in parallel with Elie Metchnikoff in Paris. I didn't hurt your sister, although I did put some of her blood through a special filter to remove certain infectious agents. If she never went home, it wasn't because of anything I did." He was by no means convinced that that was true, even if his memory could be trusted in its conviction that Caroline Dean had not been the girl who had died, but he hoped that he sounded believable, and that his word as a man of science might carry some weight with the seaman.

"And who's he?" Dean demanded, meaning Sir Julian.

"He's my patron," Mathieu said, carefully refraining from supplying a name. "He's also my patient—which is to say, one of my experimental subjects. As you can see, no harm has come to him by virtue of his involvement in my work."

"I've rarely seen a man in such good trim," the seaman admitted, suspiciously. "What are you treating him for—the pox?"

"That's not your concern," Sir Julian put in. "If I put down the gun, will you put down the knife, so that we can discuss the matter as civilized men?"

"It was you who uncivilized the situation in the first place," Dean pointed out. "It's not as easy to mend things as it is to break them, though. If you had nothing to hide, you'd hardly be planning to tie me up and flee to Ireland, would you?"

Silently, Mathieu cursed Julian Templeforth's loose mouth and propensity for hasty action. "You don't understand, Mr. Dean," he said. "So many people simply *don't understand*, even though the notion of drawing blood is perfectly familiar in medical practice. My syringes are neater and safer by far than leeches or cupping, but hollow needles still seem to intimidate the popular imagination, and the mere concept of experimentation seems to send shivers down the backs of many common folk. Have you any idea of the abuse that Louis Pasteur, the greatest benefactor of humanity this century has seen, has had to endure in the course of his researches, for his temerity in regarding the human body as a legitimate object of experimental study? If you had the least conception of the persecution that Ignatz Semmelweis underwent at the hands of physicians, for proving the necessity of sterile technique and demonstrating that they were infecting their patients with mortal diseases, you would not be in the least surprised that I prefer to work in secret, or that those who depend on my work might be a trifle over-anxious to preserve that secrecy.

"I am working for the betterment of the human condition, Mr. Dean, and would far rather do so in the open—but I need blood to feed my investigations, which no one is willing to supply but whores. If some misfortune really has befallen your sister, it was most likely the result of some infection that might have been curable two hundred years ago, if only the Age of Reason had been allowed to extend its viewpoint to the human body. If you want to blame someone for her misfortune, blame the acolytes of ignorance, superstition and horror who have surrounded medical research with all manner of prohibitions!"

Mathieu felt the pressure of the knife-point relax somewhat, and knew that he had made an impact of sorts. The seaman was no fool; whether or not he had ever heard of Pasteur and Semmelweis, he could follow the gist of the argument.

Sir Julian, on the other hand, was still pointing the gun as if he were avid to use it. The cut on his cheek was not serious, but he was exceedingly sensitive about his appearance, and he was not a man to take such an insult gracefully.

"Listen!" Mathieu said, speaking to them both. "There is, I think, a way to set Mr. Dean's mind at rest. Let him witness the treatment for which you came here tonight, my lord. Let him see that there is nothing to fear in the mere process of drawing blood and reinserting it into the body. Let him see, at any rate, that *you* are not afraid, and that you trust me to work in your best interests. Then perhaps, we can all agree that there is nothing sinister going on here, let alone anything diabolical."

Sir Julian only needed a few seconds to see the wisdom of the move, if only as a temporary delay. He had, after all, already offered, albeit in a somewhat cavalier fashion, to put his gun away in order that he and Dean might discuss matters like civilized men. "I'm agreeable to that," he said—but he flashed a warning glance at Mathieu, as if he were afraid that the scientist might give away too much.

Thomas Dean was evidently curious. "All right," he said. "I'll settle for that, for now."

4.

After a little further discussion, Sir Julian agreed to deposit his revolver on the coat-stand in the hall, while Thomas Dean placed his knife on a shelf in the laboratory. Then there was a pause while Mathieu closed and locked his front door. He took time then to inspect the cut on Sir Julian's cheek, which he sealed as carefully as he could and dressed with gauze.

"It might open again when I replace your blood, because of the anti-clotting agent," he said, anxiously, "but you should be able to staunch the flow without overmuch difficulty."

"It's only a scratch, damn it!" the baronet said. "Better a little bleeding than go without the treatment."

The seaman watched, with evident fascination, as Mathieu sat the baronet down in the chair that had recently been occupied by Judy Lee, and carefully inserted the hollow needle into his right forearm. Sir Julian did not flinch, although it was becoming far harder to connect with his veins than it had been to get into the girl's. From the corner of his eye, Mathieu saw the seaman bite his lip in sympathy. He switched on the pump that would assist the extraction.

Mathieu had set aside the apparatus that had circulated Judy's blood through the filtration matrix, having already abstracted the filtrate from the matrix. The filtrate was now being maintained in solution in a few milliliters of fresh blood, held in a rotating flask dipped in lukewarm water-bath. That was necessary because the agent lost its properties if it were completely isolated from its natural environment. When Mathieu had drawn off half a liter of Sir Julian's blood he put it in a second flask, which had already been warmed to body-temperature in the same water-bath. He detached the first flask, added the small sample of enhanced blood to the larger quantity, and then set the second flask to rotate.

"My patron's blood-type is such that he can receive blood of any other type without an adverse reaction," Mathieu said to Thomas Dean, "but it would not matter if there were some slight reaction, because the transfer of the agent is not dependent on compatibility. The agent does, however, require dilution before reinjection, in order that its effects may be properly generalized."

"What effects?" Dean understandably wanted to know.

"Increased resistance to certain innate infections," Mathieu said, employing deliberate circumlocution.

"That doesn't make sense," Dean protested. "How can taking blood from a sick child-whore—and I saw the girl who was brought here this afternoon, Mr. Galmier, so I know that she was sick—help increase resistance to disease in a healthy man?"

"It may seem strange," Mathieu told him, smoothly, "but one of my former colleagues at the Institut Pasteur, Elie Metchnikoff, has demonstrated that the body has its own innate defenses against infection. The reason that Jenner's vaccine works, we believe, is that exposure to the relatively-harmless cowpox stimulates the production of some kind of reactive agent, which is also effective against the much more dangerous smallpox. Even when the reactive agents within a human body are fighting a losing battle, they can be filtered out and concentrated, and used to arm a healthy body against the same infections that were defeating them in their original host."

Dean was, indeed, no fool. He was able to take the argument a step further than Mathieu had assumed. "And what effect does the removal of the reactive agents have on the *original hosts*?" he demanded, after only a moment's thought. "Does it not weaken them, and hasten them on heir own way to death?"

"We think not," Mathieu was quick to say, hoping that the lie was not transparent. "Indeed, I believe that my filtration process removes infective agents as well as reactive ones, preserving exactly the same balance as before in the donor—but the infective agents are held in the filter when the reactive agents are abstracted, and I am careful to destroy them there."

"In that case," Dean said, "If you were to reinject the separated reactive agents back into the donor...."

"Their condition would almost certainly improve," Mathieu agreed, making haste to get the half-truth out of his mouth, in order to return to safer argumentative ground, "and that is, of course, my long-term goal. The eventual aim of my research is to find a means of multiplying the reactive agents in isolation, so that they can then be redeployed, not merely in their original host or a single new host, but in a hundred or a thousand individuals. Given time, and sufficiently effective filters, we might not only put an end to dozens of infectious diseases, slow down the aging process and…." He paused in response to Sir Julian's warning glare, and then finished, a trifle lamely: "and accelerate the healing process in wounds inflicted by bullets and blades."

"I see," the seaman said, studying Sir Julian's face and figure carefully. "Well, your patient certainly looks well on the treatment—all the more so if he really does have the clap."

Sir Julian scowled at that, but Mathieu moved to fill yet another Pravaz syringe from the contents of the warm flask, and made ready to reinject the baronet's blood, hoping to distract his attention and soothe his quick temper.

"I can assure you that my patient is not suffering from syphilis or any other life-threatening disease," Mathieu was quick to say, as he connected the syringe to the needle that was still in place and began to depress the plunger.

"That's very good news," said a voice from the doorway, in a pronounced Irish brogue. "Indeed, we could hardly have hoped for better."

Mathieu, Sir Julian and Thomas Dean turned simultaneously to the man who had just stepped into the room, carrying Sir Julian's revolver carelessly in his right hand. He was as tall as Thomas Dean, and somewhat broader. Mathieu recognized the man that Dean had earlier put to flight. He was not alone, this time; he had brought reinforcements with him.

It occurred to Mathieu, somewhat belatedly, that he had locked his front door after bidding farewell to Judy Lee, and that the "sneak-thief" from whom Thomas Dean had saved him must therefore have had some way of turning the key in the lock from the far side of the door, without making any appreciable noise, other than the click of the latch when he actually opened the door.

He guessed, too, that the man who had been watching the house in Holland Park—this man or one of his companions—had not followed him *to* the house at all, although he must certainly have followed him home, in spite of all his precautions.

"Never fear," the newcomer said. "I'm no hooligan, and I've not the least intention of using this toy—although I confess that I'd rather have it in my hand just now than see it in someone else's."

"Who the hell are you?" Sir Julian demanded.

"I'm Sean Driscoll, Sir Julian, the president of your tenants' association—or *our* tenants' association, at any rate. My friends here are my deputies, Michael MacBride and Padraig Reilly. You've long been acquainted with Mr. Reilly's great-uncle, I believe, although I met him for the first time myself last night, under circumstances that were admittedly awkward. We've been engaged in talks with your steward for some time, and have urged him as powerfully as we could, but in vain, to fetch you back to our estates so that we might include you in the negotiations. Now, we're following the advice of whatever wise fellow it was who said that, if the mountain will not come to Mahomet, then Mahomet must go to the mountain—although I hasten to add that we're all good Catholics."

"Get this thing out of my arm," Sir Julian said to Mathieu, tersely. Then, to Driscoll, he said: "What on Earth do you think you're doing, coming after me here, of all places?"

"Well, sir," the Irishman said, "that's a slightly embarrassing matter—although I have to confess that we weren't sure what sort of a welcome we'd get if we rang the bell at Holland Park, even though young Padraig here is kin to your gatekeeper. The truth is that there are all kinds of rumors running around your estate, sir, about your having made a deal with the Devil, selling your soul in exchange for eternal youth. I never believed them for an instant, of course, being a man who can read and figure as well as most, but I had to admit that I was surprised when I caught sight of you last night, for the first time in twenty years. I knew your father, you see, and I had abundant opportunities to observe you in the days when you used to favor us with our presence over the water, although I doubt that you ever noticed me. I did not mistake this gentleman for the Devil, of course, even though he's a foreigner, but I *was* curious to discover what dealings you had with him. It's a wise tenant who knows his landlord, sir—especially when he has protests to lodge and polite requests to make. I'm truly glad to find that your friend is no more than a physician, and that your unnatural good looks are purely at- tributable to good health—if that really is the case."

"You've got a damned nerve," Sir Julian retorted. "I think you'll find that Irish rebels are by no means welcome on English soil, and that you'll likely end up in jail if I call the police."

"I'm not a rebel, sir," Driscoll replied, equably. "I really don't care one way or the other about Home Rule. What I do care about is justice between landlord and tenant. If I'm fairly treated, it doesn't matter overmuch whether the land I work is owned by an English- man, an Irishman or a Chinaman—but given that I'm not being fair- ly treated, in my opinion, then I feel obliged to make my position clear. You may call the police if you wish, sir—but if my guess is right, that's not something you're overly enthusiastic to do. This other gentleman sent me packing a little while ago, when I thought myself outnumbered again and made another tactical retreat, but if what I've overheard in these last few minutes is anything to go by, he has grievances of his own against you, and against your physician too. I have sisters myself, and daughters too, and I know well enough how a man's ire can be roused when he loses one, or finds one in dire straits through no fault of her own. Would it interest you to know, by any chance, Mr. Dean, that the man sitting in front of you is fifty-nine years old, and that he looked a great deal older and far less good-looking when he was thirty-and-one than he does now."

Mathieu could tell that Thomas Dean was, indeed, interested to hear that item of information, even though he did not know quite what to make of it.

While the seaman was still puzzling over the unexpected revela- tion, Driscoll handed him the revolver. "I think this had best be committed to the care of a neutral party," he said, "while my com- panions and I explain our grievances to our landlord. With all due respect to the owner of all this fine apparatus, this room seems to me to be a trifle cramped and gloomy for our purposes, so I think it might be best if we and Sir Julian removed ourselves to somewhere more comfortable—perhaps a public house if, as I suspect, he does not care to invite us to his home."

"You can get drunk wherever you please," Sir Julian said, getting to his feet now that he was no longer unencumbered by Mathieu's apparatus, a little unsteady on his feet but evidently determined to stand as firm as he could. "I have no intention of negotiating with you, on English or Irish soil. Any grievances you might have must be taken up with my steward. If you do not leave this house immediately, I shall certainly summon the police—and I think you'll find them unprepared to take your word for it that you have no rebel sympathies or criminal intentions, given that you're guilty of breaking and entering."

Sean Driscoll's florid face put on a fine show of feigned distress in response to this declaration, but Mathieu had the impression that the big Irishman had little or no idea what to do next. He was far from home, and must know very well that he would be in a weak position if his contest with an English baronet really did become an issue for English law to settle. Mathieu noticed, too, that there was now only one man standing behind him—although the two of them were just as capable of blocking the door, should they see fit to do so, as three. The man who had disappeared was the one who had been introduced as Michael MacBride.

"I broke nothing," Driscoll said, mildly. "The key was in the lock, and it has too long a shaft, allowing it to be turned from the wrong side. What you need, my friend, is a strong bolt, or a sturdy bar."

"Just a minute," said Thomas Dean, finally. "Are you saying that Dr. Galmier really has discovered an elixir of youth? That he's stealing the health from the blood of young girls and injecting it into his paymaster?"

"Well, now," Driscoll said, with a slight spontaneous smile, "Dr. Galmier's certainly not injecting it into himself, is he? Unless, that is, he's a hundred years old instead of thirty-some."

"It's not as simple as that," Mathieu was quick to put in.

"Be quiet!" Sir Julian commanded him, intemperately. "That's our business, and no one else's. All these men are trespassing, Professor, having invaded your lodgings uninvited, whether they broke your door or not. This one has held a knife to your throat and now has a gun. Will you go to Goldhawk Road, if you please, and find a policeman. Tell him to summon help, and to come armed, prepared to meet violent resistance."

Mathieu eyed the route to the laboratory door apprehensively, not at all sure that he would be allowed to walk out without meeting violent resistance himself. Nor was he sure that he wanted to leave his apparatus—but he knew that he could hardly round on the baronet and tell him to go in search of a policeman himself if he really wanted one to come. Instead, he opened his mouth to say that there was no need for any trouble, hopeful that he might be able to find further arguments to support that assertion, but he was interrupted by the noise of movement in the hallway. Padraig Reilly came further into the room as Michael MacBride reappeared in the doorway, in company with another person, who was definitely not a policeman.

It was direly difficult to tell, at first glance, exactly what the other person might be, given that he or she was clad in a capaciously-hooded cape which, in combination with a thick woolen scarf, hid every feature of the face within, save for the faint gleam of feverish eyes. Mathieu, however, was not in the slightest doubt that the person must be female. The hood testified to that even more clearly than her short stature. Set between the three burly Irishman she looked incredibly frail, even though the bulky cape blurred the sharp lines of her emaciated frame.

Mathieu's heart sank, and he had a vertiginous feeling of being utterly lost. This was by no means the first time that one of his former "volunteers" had returned in search of help, having run out of other options, and they almost always returned in this part of the evening, when the cover of darkness was fully secured but before the London streets became truly hazardous for those incapable of self-defense. He never let them past his front door, though, and none had ever come when Sir Julian was present. Cormack was the only other person involved to have set eyes on one of them, and Cormack's heart was even harder than his master's, at least in some respects. Mathieu found himself with his mouth open, in expectation of having something to say, but quite incapable of speech.

"Girl wants to see the doctor," MacBride reported, laconically. "Hadn't the heart to tell her that he was busy. Best take her to another room, though, sir, if you have one."

Mathieu felt dizzy, and feared that he was about to faint. He could not help staring at those fugitive eyes hidden in the shadows of the hood, even though he was terrified by the idea of meting their accusatory stare.

He felt a peculiar surge of relief as he realized that he did not have to do that. The gaze of the terrible eyes was not fixed on him at all but on something else—some*one* else.

Three seconds of awful, pregnant silence went by, while Mathieu observed strangely similar expressions of puzzlement forming on the faces of Sir Julian Templeforth and Sean Driscoll, neither of whom had begun to comprehend what was happening.

Then the girl spoke, and her voice, though inexpressibly feeble, struck Mathieu with all the impact of a bomb—because what she said was: "Tom? Is that you?"

Thomas Dean's Caroline, Mathieu realized, was definitely not the girl who had died. Thomas Dean's Caroline had presumably vanished from her family's ken because she simply had not been able to bear the prospect of going home. In a way, that was good news—but in another way, it was anything but good. Thomas Dean was still holding Sir Julian's revolver.

The seaman did not waste time with idle repetition of his sister's querulous question. He had a more direct means of discovering whether the girl in the hood was known to him, and he only had to take one long stride reach out his arm to push back the hood.

She flinched, reflexively. She actually raised her hands in order to try to fight him off when he tried to pull down the scarf, but she could not do it.

Mathieu anticipated the general gasp of astonishment and horror a split second before it actually sounded within the room, and the anticipation made it even worse. He stepped backwards, pressing his spine against the wall in a narrow gap between two sets of shelves.

Thomas Dean's automatic response was to exclaim: "You're not Caroline!"

The girl made no attempt to assert her identity, and seemed to be biting her bloodless lip in anguish over the fact that she had given herself away. She tried to turn and run, but MacBride and Reilly were still blocking the door, and were too stunned to remove themselves from her path.

San Driscoll swore, softly. Sir Julian's handsome face was uniformly white, save for the red stain on the dressing applied to his cut—which did not make it any less handsome, but somehow contrived to augment the insult.

"Caroline?" said Thomas Dean, helplessly, admitting the truth in spite of what must have seemed blatant evidence to the contrary. Then he raised the gun, and pointed it at Mathieu. "You did this," he said, hoarsely. "You really are the Devil."

"You don't understand," Mathieu protested, although it was obvious that everyone in the room understood the fundamental fact perfectly well, however incredible they had found the possibility when voicing it before. They had been no more able to believe in any kind of elixir of youth than they had been able to believe that Sir Julian Templeforth really had made a bargain with the Devil, despite Sean Driscoll's observation regarding the remarkable transformation of the baronet's appearance. In isolation, even given what they knew about what went on in the laboratory, that appearance had merely seemed an oddity, a strange stroke of luck. Now, juxtaposed with its counterpart, it seemed something very different, and literally diabolical.

Except, Mathieu insisted to himself, it was not diabolical at all—not literally, or even metaphorically. It was authentically hopeful: a highly significant step on the path of progress; a staging-post *en route* to the Age of Miracles. *That* was the understanding he had to convey to them—not just to the dangerous man with the revolver, but to all of them—if they would only give him time.

However dangerous he might be, however, Thomas Dean was not a stupid man. He did not squeeze the revolver's trigger, although his stance and expression suggested that he would be perfectly prepared to do so. Instead, he said: "Reverse it! Right here, right now. Take back what you stole, and return it."

Mathieu knew that he must have gone pale in his turn, but he knew how futile it was to protest when he stammered: "No...you don't understand...it doesn't work like that...." While he forced the words out, his gaze darted around the company, taking in Sir Julian and all three Irishmen before settling on Sean Driscoll's face.

Even if Thomas Dean had been alone, Mathieu thought, the gun would have given him the means of backing up his demands, although he would probably have had to put at least one bullet into Sir Julian's body to force his cooperation. The fact that he was not alone, though, increased his advantage vastly, in moral as well as material terms—and he was not alone in any sense of the term. The Irishmen were outraged on his behalf; thy shared his horror, if not his pain. They had no reason to love Sir Julian, and some reason, at least, to think that they might benefit in the short or long term were the baronet to be robbed of his unnatural virility, but even if they had had no advantage of their own at stake, they would still have sided with Thomas Dean and backed him up. They had never seen Caroline Dean before she had accepted Cormack's guinea, but they had imagination enough to assure them that she might—must—have been as pretty as any young girl on the brink of puberty. It required little or no creative effort for them to exchange, in their minds' eyes, Sir Julian's preternatural beauty for her dismal plainness, restoring her lost purity at the expense of his.

In a single visionary flash, Mathieu saw that it really was going to happen. His four unwelcome visitors really were going to force Sir Julian back into the chair, tying him down if necessary, so as to demand that Mathieu must draw out his blood, as he had drawn Judy Lee's that afternoon, and Caroline Dean's some little while ago. Then they were going to force him to inject the filtered produce of Sir Julian's blood into the girl, just as he had injected the filtered produce of Judy Lee's blood into Sir Julian mere minutes before. And he would have no choice but to do it. They would not give him a choice. If he refused, Thomas Dean would hurt him, and keep on hurting him until he complied. They had no fear of the police now; they were obedient to what they considered to be a higher law.

But they truly did not understand the finer details of the situation. They were thinking in mystical terms; they did not understand the way that the natural world was made. They did not understand that this was science, not magic, and what the harsh implications of that distinction were.

"You don't understand," he said, yet again, feeling compelled to mount what defense he could. "It won't work...." He realized even as the voiced the second phrase, though, that nothing he could say would be sufficient to persuade them. Their notion of justice out-weighed mere practical considerations. Even if he did explain, and managed to persuade them of the truth, it would not stop them. It would not stop Sean Driscoll, let alone Thomas Dean. This was the kind of nightmare that could not be escaped, from which there would be no awakening—and when it was over, what then? What would become of him—and, more importantly, of progress?

5.

Strangely, given his character, Sir Julian did not put up much of a fight. The three Irishmen subdued him easily, trussed him up and secured him to the chair—after which he did not struggle, seemingly accepting his fate. The baronet seemed to see the awful logic of the situation as clearly as Mathieu did, and to feel the weight of its narrative propriety just as forcefully; he seemed resigned, at least for the moment, to the fact that his hubristic defiance of natural destiny had finally been called to account, and that Nemesis had descended upon him.

Mathieu did not make any attempt at physical resistance either. Nor did he entertain the notion of trying to cheat, by substituting some other procedure for the one they were demanding that he carry out. He was, however, determined to make every possible effort to explain—and he could see that Driscoll, at least, was as hungry for an explanation as he was to see some result. Even Thomas Dean, who desperately wanted to see a miracle performed, was man enough to want to know exactly what had been done to his sister, and how and why. In Mathieu's estimation, too, Dean was fully enti-tled to know exactly how and why his passionately-desired miracle would fail to materialize.

Before he began work, Sir Julian whispered in his ear: "I have your money in my pocket, Mathieu. I'll get you more—as much as you need. We'll begin again, when this setback is behind us. We'll set everything to rights. This won't stop us." The baronet's voice was quivering with desperation, eager for reassurance.

Mathieu refrained from telling his patron, bluntly, that it wasn't as simple as that. It might be best, he thought if Sir Julian continued to believe, for as long as possible, that he could be restored to his present condition once this little "setback" had been put behind them.

Before he began his general explanation, though, Mathieu instructed Michael MacBride to make a large pot of tea, and asked Sean Driscoll to send Padraig Reilly out to the night-stalls in Goldhawk Road, in search of bread, meat pies and oil for the lamps.

Thomas Dean had set his ugly sister down on a kitchen chair, positioned so that she could see every detail of what happened to Sir Julian Templeforth.

The baronet groaned as the needles were inserted into his veins, and his eyes bulged with unsuppressable horror as he watched the blood begin to flow through the filtration apparatus.

"The filter," Mathieu said, calmly, to his uninvited guests, "is the key to the whole process. That was the one stroke of luck I had that might have been unrepeatable by another researcher. The removal of blood from the body, the prevention of its clotting and its reintroduction may seem bizarre to you, but they'll very soon be routine procedures in medical practice. In the twentieth century, there will be nothing in the least unusual in people selling their blood for the use of others, probably for less than the guinea Miss Dean was paid. The filter, on the other hand, is truly remarkable. At first, I hoped to make use of the orthodox filters used in chemical analysis, but I soon realized that the biological agents I was trying to sieve out are extraordinarily delicate, and very easily destroyed. Some of them, it seems, can only survive in contact with living tissue. I began experimenting with filters comprised of networks of fungal hyphae, and was fortunate enough to find one that not only trapped but preserved the agent that became the focal point of my future research.

"The whole *raison d'être* of the Institut Pasteur is to substitute a new scientific medicine for the alchemical medicine of old, and to replace the occult version of the human microcosm with an image based on the findings of microscopy and organic chemistry. We knew at the outset, of course, that the microcosm in question would not be simple, but we had no conception of the awesome extent of the complexity that we would discover—although *discover* may be too strong a word, given that we have barely begun the process of exploration. John Donne once proclaimed that no man is an island, and he was correct—for every man is, in fact, not merely an island but a universe, entire and unique, which plays host to all manner of microbiological life-forms, and other agents whose nature seems to be ambiguously suspended between life and inertia. You might have heard talk of bacilli and protozoans, but we shall require a terminology far more elaborate than that to get to grips with the complexity of the multitudinous entities that dwell within a human body, the vast majority of which remain invisible to the most powerful microscopes."

Mathieu broke off his discourse because Reilly returned with the goods he had been sent to buy. While the others set about making a frugal meal, Mathieu refilled the lamp that had gone out and lit it, bringing the room some way back from the dismal gloom that had set in. He topped up the other lamp, and turned up its flame, but the illumination the lamps provided, even at their maximum effect, had an ochreous tinge that did not make the assembled apparatus seem any less sinister.

"Thanks to Professor Pasteur," he continued, "we now know that many, if not all, diseases are caused by micro-organisms of one sort or another. Thanks to Edward Jenner, we have begun to find ways of countering the pathological activity of those invaders, sometimes by means of other micro-organisms. The vast majority of the entities that live within us are, however, benign. It is quite possible that we could not exist without them—that the life we think of as our own is actually a collaborative enterprise, and that the processes of progressive evolution that the Chevalier de Lamarck and Charles Darwin have identified and explained are collaborative too. At any rate, our internal populations are as subject to the principle of natural selection as we are, and far more intensely, by virtue of the brief life-spans of the individuals comprising them.

"When I was at the Sorbonne I agreed with my colleagues in thinking of aging and death in terms of disease. Like them, I entertained the hope that we might one day find ways to combat the disease of aging, perhaps to find a medical elixir of life. That was why I went to the Institut. Once there, though, I began to think in somewhat different terms, wondering whether it was really accurate to imagine youth and health in terms of the mere absence of, or resistance to, agents of decay. I began to wonder whether good health and the common attributes of youthfulness might more accurately be considered as positive results of the tireless endeavor of active agents, while old age and death are merely the consequences of the eventual fatigue and failure of those collaborative indwellers.

"There was nothing unreasonable about that kind of eventual failure, I realized, in terms of the logic of Darwin's theory. Like all living organisms, the primary imperative of our indwelling multitudes is to reproduce themselves, not merely within the context of a particular human microcosm but in terms of the further reproduction of the microcosm entire. Natural selection exerts strong pressure on our indwelling micro-organisms—especially those which, unlike disease-causing bacilli, cannot easily transmit themselves from one microcosm to another by infection or contagion—to do whatever they can to further the cause of human reproduction. Once the reproductive phase of human life is over, however, such micro-organisms would no longer be subject to pressure maintaining that aspect of their activity."

"Is what you're saying, sir," Sean Driscoll put in, struggling to understand in spite of his evident incredulity, "that human youthfulness and virility are actually the product of germs resident within us?"

"No," Mathieu said bluntly. "What I'm saying is that it is to the advantage of some of our indwelling micro-organisms to enhance or augment those aspects of youth and virility that facilitate human reproduction. I don't claim that any of these attributes is the creation of the passengers within our personal universes, but I do claim that there are biological agents dwelling within us which assist in the amplification of our reproductive capacities. To be specific, I claim that there are separable agents dwelling within us that make a measurable, even substantial, contribution to our sexual attractiveness."

"A bacillus of beauty!" Driscoll said, catching a glimpse of enlightenment.

"Not a bacillus, exactly, and there may be more or less at stake in physiological terms than our ready-made concept of *beauty* usually embraces—but yes, in simple terms, I'm referring a biological agent that promotes good looks. What I took from Miss Dean and gave to Sir Julian is not youth, *per se*, but the means of attractive appearance. As you observed before, I have contrived to turn an exceptionally plain man into an exceptionally handsome man."

At that point in the argument, Mathieu thought, every eye in the room should have turned to Sir Julian, who was still outrageously handsome in spite of his pallor and the fact that he was slumped in his chair, exhausted by the extended circulation of his blood. In fact, his uninvited guests looked in another direction entirely: at Caroline Dean. Instead of wanting to appreciate the glory of his achievement, they were intent on examining its cost.

So far as Mathieu could remember, Caroline Dean had not been an exceptionally good-looking girl—certainly not as ethereally beautiful as Judy, although he seemed to remember now that she had been somewhat healthier. Cormack had obviously found the Bethnal Green flesh-market a trifle understocked that day. She had been pretty enough, in her own fashion, though. She had had something to contribute to his mission—and, in consequence, something to lose. Her face was not quite the Medusal mask that her brother had appeared to perceive, even now, but she was definitely ugly. Her cheeks and chin were slack and dull; her complexion was terrible; her hair was thin and lusterless; her lips were thin and pale; her teeth were bad. Even her eyes, which still held a certain desperate gleam, were watery and colorless. Hers was not the face of a leper or a victim of vitriolization, by any means, but it was a face that she had obviously been ashamed to show to anyone who had formerly known and loved her.

That was what the Irishmen and Thomas Dean chose to look at, now that he had confirmed and explained what they had already seen for themselves. Instead of admiring the magnificent work of scientific art that was Sir Julian Templeforth, they preferred to horrify themselves by staring at the girl—one of the many girls—who had chosen freely to trade their beauty away, at a fair market price, in order to further the cause of progress.

In time, as he had insisted so frequently to Sir Julian and all his other patients, Mathieu would be able to pay them all back—if they could only survive the ravages of disease and deprivation long enough. Once he had discovered a means of reproducing the agent *in vitro*, he would be in a position to banish ugliness from the world once and for all: to make every human being alive, and all those yet to be born, as beautiful as it was possible for them to be. What a gift to humankind that would be! Was there any gift more desperately desired, more desperately needed? All that he required was time....

Except, of course, that—as he had also scrupulously pointed out—the matter was not quite as simple as that.

6.

Driscoll had untied the cords binding Sir Julian Templeforth to the chair that was set beside the filtration apparatus, and had cut the string that secured his arms and legs. He was free to get up and move away, had he so wished, but he remained where he was, utterly dispirited, while Mathieu got on with his work with all due expedition.

The representatives of Sir Julian's tenants' association might have entered into negotiations then, while they had him at something of a disadvantage, but Driscoll made no attempt to do so. It was presumably not his sense of fairness that prevented him, but his sense of now being involved in something of an altogether different order of importance. There would, Mathieu presumed, be abundant opportunity for the other kind of business later—at least, he hoped so.

Thomas Dean was now the man who felt most urgency to talk, perhaps because the revolver had begun to weight very heavily upon his hand and he had become fearful of the possibility that he might eventually be led to fire it.

"Why *him*?" he said, to Mathieu, waving the weapon's barrel vaguely in Sir Julian's direction.

"We met, quite by chance, in Paris," Mathieu told him. "He was there pursuing an *amour*—a genuine affection, not some whoring expedition. He was in love, but his feelings were not reciprocated. He had felt the burden of his plain looks for a long time, for he had a secret image of himself as a dashing cavalier, which his swordsmanship supported well enough but his face could not. He was referred to me by a mutual acquaintance who knew of my work at the Institut, with no more initial ambition than the hope that I might cure his pustulent complexion. He was a very willing subject for experimentation, and was very enthusiastic at that time to pledge his entire fortune to anyone who could make him into the kind of man he longed to be. Since he became that kind of man, alas, his attitude to his fortune and its conservation has changed somewhat."

Mathieu observed Sean Driscoll nodding sagely, although Sir Julian was scowling.

"It seems to me," Michael MacBride observed, "that you might have found a female employer far more generous and far more grateful. There's no shortage of tales of women eager to bathe in the blood of virgins to renew their beauty"

"Indeed," croaked Sir Julian. "Had he stayed in Paris, Sarah Bernhardt might have been only too pleased to employ him, even though he could do naught about her wooden leg—but you could not stay there, could you, my friend? And your career in London has not been so spotless that you could present yourself at the palace, pleading for an interview with the queen."

"I am no murderer," Mathieu retorted, quietly. "Those who died were victims of misfortune, and their own innate infections."

Caroline Dean looked up at that, and stared at him as if he had leveled some terrible insult against her, but she said nothing.

"And it does not trouble you," her brother said, in her stead, "to leech the beauty from little maids to feed some petty Anglo-Irish aristocrat with the appetites and delusions of a French dandy?"

Mathieu ignored the insult to his nationality, and thought it imprudent to point out the flagrant inaccuracy of the term "maid" in this context. "One must go to the best available source," he said, grimly. "My hope and intention has always been to increase the natural supply a thousand- or a million-fold, and eventually to render it irrelevant, so that anyone and everyone might benefit from the knowledge and the artifice. Sir Julian was as much a means to that end as your sister was."

"Well now," Sean Driscoll put in, "it seems to me, on that reckoning, that Mr. Dean might be doing you a favor just now, by increasing the range of your experiments. I'm right in thinking, am I not, that the likely result of what you've already done is that Sir Julian will revert to his natural appearance in the course of the next few days?"

Mathieu, thinking that it was necessary to play for time as well as to be hopeful, said: "Yes, that's correct."

"And when you finally stop messing about with your flasks and potions, and return what you've stolen to my sister's veins," Thomas Dean added, "she'll recover the looks she had before the *Hallowmas* left Tilbury last year?"

"It may not be as simple as that," Mathieu admitted, grudgingly, "but Mr. Driscoll is correct—it's an experiment I haven't yet attempted." Again, that was a lie.

"I need to go outside," Sir Julian stated, presumably meaning that he needed to visit the privy in the back yard. He was not asking for permission—merely explaining what he intended, in case Driscoll's men moved to stop him. No one did—but when the baronet had gone through the door Driscoll nodded to MacBride, instructing him to follow and keep Sir Julian in sight. Mathieu heard his patron go out, and then come back in a few minutes later. He judged by the consequent pattern of noises that Sir Julian had gone to the kitchen sink to wash his hands.

There was, he knew, a shaving-mirror on the kitchen wall, next to the sink. What Sir Julian would see therein in, with terror-inspired vision, Mathieu could not guess, but he felt the pressure of time upon his weary shoulders. The clock in the hall chimed twelve, each chime seeming to add a further blow to his exhaustion. He pricked up his ears, half-expecting to hear the rumble of carriage-wheels drawing up in the street outside, but there was no such noise to be heard at present. Cormack was not as strict in his punctuality when his master was not with him.

"You may sit in the chair now, Caroline," Mathieu said, with scrupulous politeness. "I'm ready to begin the infusion."

The girl was obviously frightened, but she was also hopeful. She had, after all, returned to the scene of his crime in the desperate hope that he might be willing and able to help her. She took her position while he intensified the flame of the Bunsen burner and carefully passed a hollow needle back and forth through the hottest part of the flame. He did not turn the burner down again, but removed it from beneath the lukewarm bath of water in which he had placed the blood-extract, setting the flame to heat up another bath of water, which would eventually serve to sterilize the more substantial items of his equipment.

He rubbed the girl's forearm with alcohol and inserted the needle. Then he drew off a liter of blood into a flask, which he took to the bench in order that he might process it and add the filtrate from Sir Julian blood. Silence descended on the company while he worked, uninterrupted by Sir Julian's return from the kitchen. When he set about returning the blood to Caroline Dean's veins, every eye was upon him; he felt as if he were under inspection by a flock of vultures.

"Do not expect too much too soon," Mathieu said, turning to look at Thomas Dean. "The extraction process is by no means one hundred per cent efficient. The gain is never entirely consistent with the loss. You may take her home now, though, and put her to bed. Given that he has that cut on his cheek, it will probably be best if Sir Julian stays here rather than returning to Holland Park, in order that I can keep him under observation. I have only the one bed, but you're welcome to share my vigil if you wish, Mr. Driscoll."

"Vigil be damned," Sir Julian said, less hotly than he would probably have liked. "I'm going home—and you're coming with me, Galmier. You've got what you wanted, Mr. Dean, and I'll thank you to hand my revolver back now, if you don't mind."

Sir Julian stuck out his hand, as if he had every expectation of receiving the weapon—but Thomas Dean did not surrender it.

It was during this moment of hesitation that Mathieu heard the belated sound of Sir Julian's carriage arriving to collect him. Cormack would be in the box, he knew, and there would likely be a footman behind as well as a driver. If it came to a fight now, the odds would have shifted significantly—and Sean Driscoll's expression showed that he understood that.

Mathieu saw Sir Julian take courage from that realization, and the baronet drew himself up to his full height as he turned away from the recalcitrant Dean to meet his tenant's eyes. The baronet opened his mouth, presumably to tell Driscoll and his companions that he would not meet with them, and that they must return to Ireland to air their grievances to his steward.

Driscoll was already opening his mouth too, presumably to protest that instruction—but neither man contrived to utter a word, because Driscoll's eyes suddenly betrayed astonishment, and Sir Julian read that astonishment with all the alacrity that dire anxiety could induce.

Diable! Mathieu thought. *One hour was all I needed. Just one hour!*

Sir Julian's face had begun to change. Sean Driscoll and everyone else could see it plainly—and the baronet, although he had no mirror, could read what was happening in their expressions.

This was not the slow and gradual transformation that overtook the girls who had sold their looks for a guinea. This was more reminiscent of a lycanthropic transformation, as brutal as it was sudden. It was not simply that Sir Julian's complexion became dull, or his features slack; this was a tortuous transfiguration, which erased the face of an angel with a single merciless sweep and substituted the face of a demon.

Common ugliness, Mathieu knew, really was mere plainness—a purely negative phenomenon, a mere absence—but the total absence of human beauty was no mere featurelessness. When a human face became a *tabula rasa*, it exposed the pre-human animal: the species of beast that humankind had been before human beings and their microcosmic passengers their long collaborative evolution towards naturally-selected aesthetic perfection. Sir Julian might have been ugly, as Sean Driscoll had alleged, when he was thirty-and-one years old, but he became a great deal uglier than that, now that the vast majority of his benevolent commensals had been extracted from his personal microcosm.

Mathieu had tried to leave an adequate population of the commensals behind, although he had known full well how difficult and how pointless that would be. He was not surprised by his failure, but even he was astonished by its extent and rapidity. Human beings, according to Darwin, were close kin to gorillas and chimpanzees, but the ape that Sir Julian now became was by no means as handsome as a gorilla or a chimpanzee, and the ghastly pallor of its glabrous skin only added an extra dimension to its simian awfulness.

It occurred to Mathieu—and must have occurred to Driscoll too—that Sir Julian might have a great deal of trouble henceforth persuading anyone, including his own servants, that he really was Sir Julian Templeforth.

It was impossible to judge what thoughts might have sprung into the baronet's mind, but the resultant action was obvious enough. He suddenly snatched the revolver from Thomas Dean's reluctant hand, and did his best to cover everyone as he backed through the door of the laboratory and headed along the corridor—not aiming for the front door, it seemed, but for the kitchen.

Mathieu waited, holding his breath, for the scream that would accompany Sir Julian's first sight of himself in the shaving-mirror, praying that he might hear a shot immediately afterwards as Julian proved incapable of tolerating the notion of what he had become.

There was no shot. Sir Julian Templeforth still had faith in Mathieu Galmier, and in the possibility that what had just been undone might easily be done again.

Thomas Dean, meanwhile, was staring at his sister, obviously expecting a similarly abrupt transformation that might transform her into a living angel. Nothing of the sort happened, or seemed likely to happen any time soon.

"Go!" said Mathieu, to anyone and everyone who could hear him. "For the love of God, go away! Leave me to do what I can for Sir Julian!"

No one moved to obey, but he received support from an unexpected direction when Sir Julian appeared in the doorway again, brandishing the pistol wildly, and screaming "Get out!" at anyone and everyone—except, presumably, Mathieu. The words were hardly distinguishable; clear speech was difficult for the baronet now.

Mathieu supposed that it was simply some absent-minded mechanical response that made Thomas Dean reach for the shelf where he had deposited his knife. The seaman was merely collecting his property before departing—but Dean had already thrown a scalpel at Sir Julian, and had cut him badly in the face: a wound that Sir Julian had felt as a profound insult as well as a source of pain.

Misreading Dean's intention, the baronet fired.

The ape-man's hand and eye were still sound, whatever had become of his voice; the shot struck Dean in the side of the head, and the sailor collapsed, struck dead—but he was a tall man, and a long-limbed one, and he did not fold up as neatly as he might have done. His convulsively-extended arms struck out in both directions, upsetting the Bunsen burner, the bath full of hot water, and one of the oil-lamps. A flood of flame gushed across the table.

What the intentions of the three Irishmen might have been, Mathieu could not be sure. Driscoll, at least, probably tried to disarm the baronet in a spirit of pure altruism. The others did the same, albeit more probably driven by an instinct of self-preservation. Whatever the truth of the matter, there was the immediate threat of a brawl. Sir Julian, no matter how ugly he might be, was strong and he was furious. He fired again, and again, Driscoll went down, and Reilly too, and neither was at all careful about the way that he sprawled as he fell. Broken glass flew everywhere, and the initial river of flame was scattered into half a dozen tributaries.

7.

Mathieu could not have said, afterwards, with his hand on his heart, that he kept his presence of mind. Indeed, he had no clear memory of exactly what he had done, let alone the intentions behind it.

What he actually did, though, was heroic, after a fashion. He made haste to seize Caroline Dean, plucking her thin frame out of the chair as if she weighed nothing at all, and ran for the door, cradling her like a babe-in-arms. Somehow, he got her through the doorway without tripping over anyone, living or dead, and without even smashing her head against the doorpost.

He went out the back way rather than the front, kicking the rickety back gate off its hinges rather than troubling to lift the latch. No one followed him.

He did not stop running until he reached the bushes in Ravenscourt Park, where he swiftly took shelter, collapsing in the leaf-litter to recover his breath.

Caroline was weeping. "Tom," she murmured, in a grief-stricken voice. "I've killed Tom." Seemingly, it had not yet occurred to her to blame anyone else for the train of events that her arrival in Mathieu's lodgings had precipitated.

Mathieu made a rapid estimate of the amount of flammable material contained in his laboratory, and the time it would take for a fire engine to reach the burning building. MacBride, he assumed, might well have escaped through the front door, but whether he would linger to explain to anyone what had happened, and to identify the four charred bodies that would be pulled from the ruins tomorrow or the day after, was a different matter.

"For all that anyone knows," he told the girl, "I'm probably numbered among the dead. They'll work out easily enough that Sir Julian was there, but they'll readily assume that he died as handsome as he went in. Whether or not they'll be able to put names to the others might not matter at all. If only Sir Julian had handed over the money he brought, I could be back in France within three days—or Belgium, given that it might be unwise to return to Paris."

The girl was not listening. By the not-so-distant light of a street-lamp in Paddenswick Road he could see that she was touching her face, perhaps wondering if and when it might be possible to go home again.

"Miracles only work one way, I fear," he told her, in a sincere spirit of apology. "Destruction is easy; restitution is hard. In a fairer world, there would be a balance in these matters, but Nature's notion of a balance is by no means egalitarian. The owl's delight in making each of its nightly meals is poor compensation for the agony of the mouse that has to die to provide it."

"Beauty is a delicate and costly prize, my dear, or millions of years of natural selection would have made it a far more common commodity than it is. The increase in Sir Julian's handsomeness was hard-won, requiring a kind of continual predation similar to that which sustains the owl in the ceaseless struggle for existence. It's not just the inefficiency of the process of extraction and filtration, although much potential is certainly lost therein. The agent is alive, you see, and each unique strain, being the product of a single human microcosm, cannot help but compete against others of its kind.

"The introduction of the alien strains into Sir Julian's microcosm was far from problematic. As you saw just a little while ago, his original native population had been gradually obliterated by the sequence of invasions, so that the removal of a substantial fraction of the warring factions that remained to him resulted in a rapid and total collapse of his internal equilibrium.

"I wish with all my heart that I could promise you that his loss will be matched by your gain, but that will not be the case, alas. Your own internal equilibrium has been disturbed, with no prospect of any but a temporary recovery. Yes, you might recover something distantly akin to your former prettiness in a few days' time—but it will not last, and its inevitable collapse will surely leave you even worse off than you are now.

"Had I a fully-equipped laboratory, an abundance of time and a lavish supply of funds, I would be able to help you—and I *would* help you; make no mistake about that. I would, because it has never been any part of my intention to do any lasting harm to anyone—but the path of progress is a thorny one. Unless and until I can find a means of cultivating the agent outside the human body, and growing it in unlimited quantities, more harm than good will accrue from my research. Only think, though, what the fruits of my eventual success will be! Imagine the world when beauty can be mass-produced, when ugliness will be banished forever, when self-satisfaction will be universal!

"Imagine, if you can, what an Age of Miracles the twentieth century will be, when I have succeeded in my quest—not merely for men like Sir Julian Templeforth but even for the likes of you and me! You will have played your part in that, Caroline Dean, no matter what might happen to you tomorrow, next week or next year. You will have played your part, and all humankind will thank you."

"Poor Tom," the girl murmured, still bewildered and half-delirious. "You killed poor Tom."

"Not I, child," Mathieu assured her. "I am no murderer, nor have I ever been. I am the life of the world that is to come, the seed of the glorious future. Fortunately, given what we have just endured, I'm alive, without a scratch upon me—and while I'm alive, hope is alive too, for the future of humankind. I don't know, at present, where my next meal is coming from, but I shall not be destitute for long. If Destiny protects anyone, it will surely protect me."

Feeling fully recovered, Mathieu Galmier got to his feet then, and looked around the park, wondering which way he ought to go in order to find the favor of Destiny. He was not the sort of person, though, to abandon even the most accidental of acquired responsibilities.

He put out his hand so that the girl might take it, so that he might give her the continued benefit of his protection.

She took it. She had, after all, sought him out in the hope that he might be able to help her. She had not expected to find her brother in his house, and could not be grateful fact the fact that her once-beloved Tom had seen her face, as it now was. She was more than ready to accept Mathieu's offer of succor, and to put her trust in his knowledge, his ambition and his dreams.

Besides which, the scientist thought, there was still a slim chance that she might be useful to him—at least for a fortnight or so.

KALAMADA'S BLESSING

There was once an earthly king named Kalamada, who believed—as even petty kings are wont to do—that his armies were uncommonly vast and powerful, and that his empire was a marvelous one, of greater magnificence than any there had ever been before or ever would be again. But Kalamada ruled an ignorant and primitive people, who thought that there was no other world but theirs and that the stars were put in the sky to light their way at night, and who had no notion of progress at all. Neither he nor any of his subjects could begin to imagine the might and grandeur of those empires which were yet to come upon the earth, let alone those which would one day span the worlds of many stars.

Kalamada was served by many wizards, who laid claim—as wizards are ever enthusiastic to do—to reputations of unprecedented cleverness and power. And so it happened that when his queen gave birth to an heir—as queens are bound to do—he summoned these magicians and bade them work a mighty spell, which would make the child a gifted and a lucky one.

"Wealth my son shall have, by right of inheritance," said Kalamada, "and power too—and because he hath such a comely mother, and such a proud and handsome father, he shall undoubtedly be handsome in his turn, and quick of wit. But I beg that all the power of wizardry might be brought to bear in granting him that which he cannot have by any other means: the strength of constitution to resist all fevers and diseases, and all the wounds which he might suffer in the course of a lifetime."

And this, the wizards did—or said that they had done.

* * * * * * *

When Karadak, the son of Kalamada, grew to be a man he proved indeed to be the most handsome of his race, and the quickest of wit. As the prince of the realm he lacked for nothing, save only for those things of which his people were quite ignorant, and which he had not the imagination to want. His health and strength soon became a legend, for he seemed immune to all contagion, and in the twenty-and-one years which passed in bringing him to the full flower of maturity he never suffered a single hour of ague or aching. He led his father's armies into three great battles, was victorious in each and every one, and was never wounded.

It is, however, an unfortunate fact that legendary reputations may attract attention the bounds of a single nation, and some say that it is possible for such news to be carried beyond the bounds of the universe of space and time, which contains many millions of worlds and billions of nations. Perhaps, in due course, the tale of Karadak's unyielding good health was carried to the slimy ears of the god of plague and pestilence himself, who was ever one to relish a challenge to his power.

Whether or not they were sent by that gloating god, there fell upon the land which was ruled by Kalamada a veritable welter of plagues. Pestilence shriveled the crops within the fields, and slaughtered the herds upon the hills, and slew the faithful soldiers of Kalamada's armies more prolifically than any enemy nation had ever contrived to do. And in the end, a frightful fever brought Kalamada himself to his deathbed, covered in vile sores and vomiting black bile.

Through all of this, Karadak alone remained untouched, without a single twinge of pain or thrill of nausea. He ascended in his turn to the throne of his petty empire, the all-powerful ruler of a ravaged and ruined land. It seemed that his father's magicians had done their work well—but they too were dying like flies, unable to do for themselves what they had done for Karadak.

While the plagues continued their debilitating course, Karadak wept for his father, and his armies, and his people—but in the course of time his melancholy was lifted, for he fell in love with a beautiful girl whose name was Syrana. Syrana loved him as deeply as he loved her, and brought him such joy that for a while he would not have cared had the vault of heaven itself become a fever-pit in which a creeping blight put out the very stars.

Amid all the confusion which beset the land, Karadak's happiness was inviolate and inviolable—until the day came when Syrana caught a kind of dysentery, and began to waste away. For a little while, it appeared that she might recover, but then her skin began to blacken and tumors made her belly swell, and in the end she died in dreadful agony.

Karadak, whose skin was still as pure as cream, who had never known the trivial shock of a cough or the tiny misery of a blister, felt that his own heart was broken, and wept with bitter anguish.

In the extremity of his despair, Karadak cried out to the uncaring stars which lit the night of his world, saying: "Oh my father, why didst thou not command thy wizards to keep me from the worst and most profound of weaknesses, whose name is love—for that dire failing hath given the god of plague and pestilence the one and only lever which he needed to destroy me, and with it he hath brought me sickness of heart and the certainty of death!"

And that ridiculous vanity which still possesses all the petty kings of all the petty empires of all the insignificant worlds of the illimitable universe made Karadak believe with all his heart that there never was or ever would be a man as miserable as he!

THE SHEPHERD'S DAUGHTER

Gotthard could not stop trembling. When he sat down on the crude chair, and rested his arms upon the surface of the table he felt a little better, but still his hands quivered until he pressed them together. He had not been long in Holy Orders, having taken his final vows only four years ago, in 1511; he had not learned the powers of self-control that his elder brethren had developed in order to carry forward the never-ending war against the Devil. His face was very white, but the stare which he directed at Magnus the shepherd was as hard as the black stone whose sharp ridges beribboned the poor turf of the Carpathian foothills.

"Tell me," he said to the sobbing Magnus, the words grating in his throat. "Tell me what this means."

And Magnus, who clearly felt that he had been alone with his anguish for too long, told him everything.

"She was such a pretty girl, Father, my little Hilda. She was so lovely and full of life, so very happy. She should not have been a shepherd's child at all, but the daughter of gentlefolk who could have given her all the things which I longed to give her, but could not. Her mother died when she was still very young, but I could find no other wife, nor even a housekeeper to tend my lonely hut, though I looked for one in Ruthenia as well as my native land.

"We were everything to one another, my daughter and I. She was so meek and uncomplaining that I came to believe that God must have sent her to teach me to be more content with the rough and meager life which He, in His mysterious wisdom, had shaped for me. I had always been a mild man, father, and had tried as best I could to love God, but when the storms played among the mountains and I had not enough to eat I could not help but lament the burden of my misfortunes. It was Hilda who saved me from the sin of despair, and taught me to accept that our lives, meager as our comforts might seem, were worth living. When she was old enough to do it she cooked for me and tended the fire, and helped me search in the snow for lost sheep, and was ever by my side for the lambing.

"When rumors of the breathing sickness first spread through the land I was not inclined to be anxious, for shepherds live high on the hills and our kind is not often visited by agues and fevers. But when my neighbors told of other hill-dwellers struck down, and when the murrain spread among my flock, I became afraid.

"I prayed to God and the Blessed Virgin that the trouble might be brought swiftly to its end, and I know that Hilda prayed likewise. She was so very good that, for a while, I thought it certain that Jesus and the saints must hear and heed her plea. But the animals continued to die, and those few lambs which contrived to be born in the spring were strangely deformed, so that I could no longer doubt that some dark and dreadful force was at work in opposition to our prayers.

"I heard that in the villages round Bardeyov a company of witches had been found by the good Dominicans, and were to be burned when the full extent of their evil had been properly measured. When I heard this, my hope that the plague would soon die out was renewed. But the more witches were burned, the more were found, and still the sickness cast its shadow upon the realm—and I knew that Satan and his minions must have freer rein here than ever I had suspected. The curse upon my flocks was not lifted, and when the greater number of my ewes lay dead, my beautiful Hilda began to show signs of the breathing sickness.

"Such a terror then took hold of me that I would have sold my very soul to save her, had Satan appeared to offer me his bargain— but Satan did not appear, and I devoted all my energies to the business of keeping her warm and well-fed. Alas that I could not do it better, for such blankets as I possess have not sufficient warmth to keep the chilly winds at bay, and with the wealth of my flocks melting away by the day I had naught to feed her but mutton stew and half-spoiled turnips.

THE RETURN OF THE DJINN, BY BRIAN STABLEFORD * 61

"I prayed to God and all the saints, Father, as fervently as I could, but I knew that I had not been a good enough man to be granted any wishes, and I dare say that my prayers were twisted by my anguish into an errant form. When my prayers to God went unanswered, I was led by my extremity to call upon Satan instead, saying: take another, but not my little Hilda; harrow every child in the land with the malevolence of your will, but spare mine, spare my only beloved!

"It was wrong to do it; I know that it was wrong, but I could not help myself. God had not answered, despite that the Dominicans labored so hard to save the souls which Satan had corrupted, and I could not help but feel that if Satan's empire was secure in the land, then his sovereignty was best acknowledged.

"But Satan was no more inclined than God to answer my cries for help, and I felt utterly alone, in a world as dark as any Hell, forsaken by fortune and lost in the deep well of my bitter wrath."

The shepherd paused, stifling a sob, and looked at Gotthard as if challenging him to pass judgment. Gotthard felt some constriction in his own throat, but he suppressed it, maintaining his composure.

"Go on, my son," he said, uncomfortably aware of the absurdity of addressing such words to a man six or eight years older than himself.

"Hilda grew worse with every day that passed," continued the distraught shepherd. "The fever grew in her and that dreadful coughing seemed sure to burst her heart. Every breath she took was ragged and harsh; try as she might, she could not draw air enough into her choking lungs. I bathed her head and tried to feed her mutton soup, but she could hold no nourishment within her, and the heat that possessed her flesh could not be soothed by the cold water on her brow. I could only hold her while she coughed, and I wept to see the blood which was mingled with the fluid.

"On the fifth night of her illness she died...and all my prayers were turned to terrible curses, which I hurled at Satan and his demons, and likewise at God and all his angels, for there had been no help for my darling Hilda from any of them, and there was naught but bitterness in my heart and in my soul.

"The next day, a traveler came along the ridge, heading for the village. He would have hurried by, for he was loath to enter any house with the plague so widespread in the land, but I begged him to pause. I told him of my loss, and pleaded with him to help me bury my child.

"He consented, but when he saw her lying on her bed he turned to me with a strangely dreadful light in his eye, and said that I was a wicked man, and hastened on his way.

"I watched him go, and then I went to my poor dead Hilda, to look at her once more before I began to make a grave for her myself—but I found to my horror that she was not where I had left her.

"I ran from the house, and looked wildly about, and saw her on the hillside yonder, walking in a very stiff and difficult manner.

"I ran after her, and easily caught up—and when I looked into her poor dead sightless eyes I knew that some malefic daemon had been sent from Hell to claim her corpse for the legions of the dancing dead, in order to punish me for the wrath which I had vented in my curses.

"I seized my poor dead darling and carried her back to my house, where I laid her on the bed again, and I quivered in fear of the forces which my curses had awakened. I knew that I ought to pray for forgiveness, but somehow I could not bring myself to do it, for so very many of my prayers had gone unanswered. I laid Hilda upon her deathbed once again, and tied her limbs so that she could not be taken away, but there was no more time to dig a grave that evening, and so I sat with her instead, watching the demon within her tease her poor dead limbs with jerks and twitches.

"When I finally crept to my bed I slept very deeply, because my anguish had robbed me of rest for so many nights that I was utterly exhausted. But when I woke in the morning, the cords with which I had bound my Hilda's corpse were bitten through and she was gone.

"I went searching for her, but I could not find her on the hillside, and by the time I caught up with her she had succeeded in making her way to the outskirts of the village. I could not abide the thought that the people there might see what an abomination she had become, and I tried to steal her away covertly—but half a dozen laborers and their wives came from their cottages, and while I wrestled with the demon-haunted body of my daughter they looked on with such horror that I could hardly bear their gaze.

"Though they called after me in alarm, I ran away, with that struggling demonic obscenity which had been my beautiful Hilda clutched tightly in my arms.

"Again I bound her body to the bed, but I knew that I must keep ceaseless watch over her lest the necrophiliac demon that had taken possession of her sent her off on her ghastly journey yet again. Her face was very grey by now, and though the spring had not yet turned to summer I knew that the flies which love putrescent flesh would be very anxious to discover her and swarm about her being.

"When a man I had long thought to be my friend came from the village to ask what had been the cause of the morning's commotion I asked him to fetch a priest who would help me commit my beloved's body safely to the ground and a Dominican to exorcise the demon which had come to inhabit it—and when I showed him what the demon had done to my little darling he could not conceal his horror and revulsion, and said immediately that he would send for the help which I needed.

"All through last night I was obliged to keep my vigil over the demon-haunted wreck of my beloved, for that spawn of Satan was exceedingly clever. Her poor fingers were so racked and torn that the flesh was all-but-stripped from the bone, and though her teeth had loosened in her jaw as the gums rotted away she kept trying to bite through the cords which bound her down. I had to put a strap about her neck and bind it to the bedpost very tightly, while the demon inside her ranted and raved at me in some loathsome and detestable tongue which I could not understand.

"I tried to pray, but I could not do it, for the demon's babblings filled my head and would not let me bring order to my thoughts. When I gave voice, it was to an inarticulate howling which the wolves upon the hills were not ashamed to answer.

"When morning came at last, I could see the tiny worms moving within her flesh, which was becoming very pulpy beneath the darkening skin. I knew that it would not be long before they devoured her, leaving naught behind but a whitened skeleton—and how I feared to watch that skeleton dance a bony jig upon my floor, to mock my hopelessness.

"I have been in such agony while I have waited for you to come, Father, that you cannot begin to understand my suffering. I could never have dreamed, until I was forced to watch it, what a pitiable calamity it can be to see the forces of corruption working within the helpless husk of one whose soul has fled. We are commanded to love one another, father, and whatever difficulty I may have had in following the other commandments I surely loved my beautiful daughter well enough. But where there is infinite love, father, there is also an infinite capacity to be hurt, and Hell has nothing in its seven circles which can torment me more than I have been tormented in these last few days.

"I beg you, Father, to assist me now. Implore God to give you strength to put the wicked demon from her body, and when you have done it, help me to dig a grave in which my Hilda's might rest in peace, while her soul is safe in Heaven."

Gotthard watched as the weeping man seemed to crumble in upon himself, and wondered whether he ought to weep himself. He did not know what to do, or what to believe. He sat for a few moments in silence, restlessly fingering his rosary, and then he crossed himself.

"Magnus," he said, finally. "Your daughter still lives. Despite that she is near to starving...despite her snapped and twisted fingers...despite the bruises about her face and legs...and despite that strangling cord which you put about her neck, she lives. She is calling for you now, though she is so sorely hurt that can raise no more than a very faint whisper. Go to her, my son, and I will pray that she might yet be saved."

Magnus ceased weeping then, and fixed the hapless priest with a stare more wrathful than any that Gotthard had ever seen before.

"Vile man!" the shepherd cried, "Is every living being within this misbegotten realm a servant of Satan, sent to increase the horror of his torments? She is dead, I tell you—dead and demon-haunted, because I could not help but curse that cruel and answerless God to whom I prayed. Come with me, man, and see! Only see, with honest eyes, and the truth will be manifest! Tell me when you have seen through the veil of demonic illusion, *is she not dead?*"

Gotthard suffered himself to be drawn again by the tortured shepherd to the bed where his daughter lay.

"See!" shrieked Magnus, seizing a handful of his own hair as though he might tear it from his head. "Is she not dead? Tell me the truth, is she not dead?

It was with the greatest difficulty that Gotthard tore his eyes away from the shepherd's pain-racked face, which had in it all the misery and blindness of the damned, to look down at the bruised and broken body of the little girl, who was silent now.

She was so wretchedly thin that it was impossible to believe that she had ever been beautiful.

The priest touched his fingers to the girl's brow, and then picked up her tiny hand, and let it fall again. "Aye," he said, while a heavy melancholy took possession of his heart, "she is dead—now."

SHADOWS OF THE PAST

PREFACE

So far as modern legend knows, the first European colony to be founded on the continent beyond the Western Ocean was established by the Cymric Prince Madoc. The Cymri were, however, just as inclined as every other race to rework their legendary heritage in order to magnify their own mythic role. Almost all of what the Cymri claimed as their own belonged to their ancestors, the Breizh, whose civilization was greater by far before the Great Cataclysm that sank the city of Is and the great forest of Lyonesse.

The abundant writing that the Breizh produced before the Cataclysm was couched in an alphabet whose symbols were lost even before the last fragile documents on which it was inscribed finally rotted away, so the few examples that remained when the Phoenicians invented the modern alphabet were unreadable. That did not prevent the fanatical scribes of the great library of Alexandria from copying the Breizh documents they contrived to discover, but far the greater number of the surviving copies were lost in one or other of the fires that devastated the library's stock before Alexandria's turn came to be inundated by a new Catastrophe. Only one such document was ever translated into a modern script, and the translation in question must be regarded as speculative, given that it was an exercise in cryptography carried out without the aid of any analogue of the Rosetta stone.

Even the accuracy of that secondary document's translation into English must be reckoned somewhat dubious, but whatever distortions have infected it, it remains a unique shadow of a lost, and perhaps not entirely inglorious, past.

1.

To Whom It May Concern,

I cannot tell whether this record will ever be recovered from the stream into which I must cast it, sealed in a glass bottle. I know that the stream will carry it eastwards through the canyons of the Mountains of Mourning to some confluence where the nameless tributary empties in the great river that flows past the mighty citadel of Marakand. There, with luck, some loyal servant of King Luthal might see it floating past and have sufficient curiosity to gather it in. If not, and it passes with the river's flow into the Sea of Sorrows, I shall have to hope that the tide might eventually wash it up on the southern shore, near to the citadel of Arganet.

If that opportunity too is lost, then I pray that the bottle might sink to the ocean floor, or be carried south to the lands of the lycanthropes, so that—at the very least—its contents can bring no comfort to our present enemies.

* * * * * * *

My name is Porphyran. I was born in Nagda, a town overfull of witches and petty sorcerers. Being of direly ignoble birth, I was put into service at an uncomfortably early age, but was fortunate enough to be taken into the employ of Alannah Sethyvys, a studious sorceress and dutiful follower of a Beast-God whose name I must not write, but whose Sacred Passion was Wrath—not random wrath, of course, but righteous Wrath, which serves the cause of justice, and hence of Symmetry, rather the cause of destruction, and hence of Chaos.

Given that detail of her religion, which some might consider unpropitious, Alannah Sethyvys was a good enough mistress, who rarely had me beaten, and was moderate in her use of insults even though I was a clumsy child who must have tried her patience sorely. She taught me to read and write in order that I might assist her in her studies and the recording of her investigations.

Unlike the majority of her kind, Alannah Sethyvys was not much given to the dispensation of poisons and love-potions, having inherited sufficient wealth from her grandmother to devote herself to scholarly research. Nor was she any mere experimenter, forever brewing potions and feeding them to rats and toads in order to judge their lethal potential; she was a lover of ancient books and scrolls, dedicated to the preservation and recovery of neglected formulas and rituals, which might otherwise have fallen into the abyss of forgetfulness.

I do not know how much I need to explain to the intended recipient of this message, but at the risk of repeating common knowledge, I ought perhaps to explain that, unlike the shapeshifting sorcerers of Marakand and Arganet—who are organized into guilds, each one attached to the temple of a particular Beast-God—the witches of the outlands are usually solitary individuals devoid of any power of metamorphosis. They regret their incapacity, but the invariance of their flesh is compensated by an unusual suppleness of mind, which assists them in the work of shapereading. Although quite unable to transform themselves, they do have the power to discover omens and specters in smokes and vapors, which serve their intuition as suggestive oracles.

Shapereaders cannot work in the confines of a fortress-city because the air is as crowded as the streets; the produce of thousands of cooking-fires and kettles mingles there with the output of an even greater number of hookahs and clay pipes. Shapereaders need their own space, and their own atmosphere. Even so, their findings are often valuable to kings, princes and merchants, revealing future opportunities and warning of future dangers. For this reason, the work of witches like Alannah Sethyvys is not without a definite prestige within the walls of the great citadels.

The research undertaken by my mistress was particularly concerned with the interpretation of a category of smokeshapes that witches call "ultraserpentine" or "cryptosaurian". These mysterious manifestations had puzzled her fellow shapereaders for many generations, various interpreters disagreeing as to whether they ought to be reckoned omens, specters or chimeras. Omens, in the theory of shapereading, are inanimate signs displayed by the generosity of the better gods; specters are the echoes of living entities; chimeras are the products of errors made by the magicians who invoke the relevant smokeshapes.

Specters are usually recognizable by virtue of the fact that their shapes correspond to those of familiar Beast-Gods: bats, bears, wolves and so on. Ultraserpentine shapes have no such resemblance, but some witches believe that they might still be specters, on the assumption that other Beast-Gods were recognized in the distant past as symbols of the spectrum of Sacred Passions. A few—among whose number was Alannah Sethyvys—believe that sorcerers who appear to lack the power of shapeshifting have simply lost contact with the images that once determined their transformations, and with the Sacred Passions those gods represented. Scholars of this persuasion believe that witches might be able to recover the skill of metamorphosis if only they can re-establish fruitful contact with the neglected gods. Whether that is true or not, generations of scholarly witches have pored over their continually-updated records of ultraserpentine manifestations, either in the hope of recovering the spectral image of some lost Beast-God or in the hope of detecting meaningful patterns within the supposedly-ominous sequence of their appearances.

The far-traveling Breizh who were our august ancestors were by no means the first inhabitants of this troubled continent, and the witches of Nagda have discovered fragments of ancient clay tablets strewn among the rocks of the Withering Waste, on whose edge the town stands. Although it is difficult in the extreme to piece these fragments together in such a way as to reveal extensive scripts, Alannah Sethyvys was convinced that some few of these tablets contained records of shapereadings, admittedly gnomic in character, written long before our ancestors first arrived on this unexpectedly hospitable shore of the Sea of Sorrows, after crossing the Almighty Ocean.

My mistress believed, on the basis of certain fragments she had contrived to decipher, that the enigmatic shapereadings recorded on the shattered tablets were specifically and exclusively concerned with shapes of the ultraserpentine or cryptosaurian variety. After long intellectual and imaginative endeavor, she convinced herself that if only she could find even one entire tablet, she would be able to settle the disagreement as to whether the shapes in question were ominous, spectral or chimerical in nature. She preferred the spectral hypothesis, of course, but she was a sufficiently conscientious scholar to be able to content herself with an unpalatable truth, provided that she could prove it.

It was for this reason that Alannah Sethyvys became determined to undertake a westward expedition into the mountainous heart of the Withering Waste, where certain relics of a settlement antedating the first arrival of our ancestors had lately been observed by explorers in search of a navigable route to the continent's far shore. As her faithful secretary and assistant, I was a vital member of the expedition, in spite of my manifest lack of humbler practical skills.

2.

When we set out, we were a company of eight. There were three other male servants in addition to myself, and Alannah Sethyvys had hired three guides who had served with earlier expeditions. We were well-equipped, and we experienced no serious problems while we were moving across the plain towards the uplands, even though the journey was long and tedious.

Unfortunately, the weather turned bad almost as soon as we began to climb into hills of a more forbidding sort. Food became hard to purchase and even harder to gather, and our guides' knowledge of the terrain proved to be very vague. The slopes were often treacherous, the low gullies being subject to sudden floods when the rain fell in torrents, as it often did.

The journey became increasingly arduous, but there was a further stage in which its perils were entirely ordinary, so I shall pass over that phase swiftly, saying only that we lost the three other serving men and one of the guides, one by one, to disaster and disease. By the time we finally reached the relics of the ancient settlement—at which point our remaining guides felt free to desert us—I was Alannah Sethyvys' sole companion. By this time there were no native farmers or herdsmen from who we could obtain food easily, and I have to admit that such expertise as I had been able to cultivate in the arts of hunting and gathering were very meager. Had it not been for my mistress's magic, which assisted me in matters of fortunate discovery and trapping game, we would likely have starved. We were, however, able to proceed with our quest.

We eventually arrived on a high and narrow plateau, pitted with deep crevices and surrounded by wind-blasted crags. A more inhospitable spot would have been hard to imagine, but the rainwater that washed over the plateau was caught and held by a thousand scar-like pools, and twisted trees clung to cracks where the dust had accreted over centuries to form a soil of sorts. No grasses grew there, but there were numerous plants of a bulbous and spiky kind, and the trees put forth purple fruit on which the big black birds that haunted the region gorged themselves. My first impression of the place was that it might once have been suitable for the habitation of lesser beings than ourselves—simians or troglodytes—but could not possibly have been fit even for fully-human folk, let alone for shapeshifters.

Knowing, as I had been educated to believe, that troglodytes prefer to live inside mountains rather than on their outer faces, my first estimation was that the remnants of ancient stone buildings which could be seen on some of the steeper crags were likely to have been troglodyte-nests—but I suspected even then that they might not be the produce of any race that still exists.

"It will not be easy to reach those ruins, Mistress," I said, when we had taken a long look around, having come on to the plateau in mid-afternoon, "and I cannot see that any one of them looks more promising than the rest. I doubt that we'll find shelter tonight."

"That's because you're a miserable fool, Porphyran," Alannah Sethyvys told me, "with eyes so poor that a human being should be ashamed to own them. Spoiled as my own sight is by too much reading, I can see still traces of the paths that might take us up into the heights. The houses whose outer walls have fallen into rubble might once have had cellars, or inner chambers hollowed from the rock, that will provide adequate lodgings."

Sighted or not, she had to close her eyes and draw upon the hidden resources of a magician to select a direction and a destination, but she had always had a good instinct in such matters and I had to assume that she made the wisest selection possible.

Darkness had fallen on the plateau before we reached the spot my mistress had picked out, but we climbed fast enough and high enough to keep the rim of the sun in sight as it sought concealment beneath the western horizon. The air in the mountains is supposed to be clean as well as cold and thin, but the central mountains of the Withering Waste are not so high that one can see what lies beyond their western neighbors. There was more than enough airborne dust in the west to turn the face of the sun blood-red, and the sky around it a delicate shade of purple.

Because the sun's stained light seemed to be coming at us from below rather than above, and because the slopes up which we scrambled were oddly curved as well as slanted, the shadows we cast were the strangest I had ever seen. They were huge and weirdly distorted, deep blue in color. I am short of stature even by the meager standards of our race, but Alannah Sethyvys was unusually tall and her shadow was a veritable giant, which moved in an impossibly elastic fashion to match her tentative footsteps, like some eldritch stalker.

When we arrived at the particular ruin selected at a distance by my mistress we found that it did not, after all, contain a cellar, nor any chamber let into the rock. Luckily, its walls had not entirely collapsed or crumbled away, and their remnants sheltered us from the worst effects of the wind. There was also a dead tree nearby, which gave us firewood. I doubt that we could have lit a fire in that frosty wind without the aid of a witch's magic, but Alannah Sethyvys was as expert in the art of ignition as she was in the art of shapereading.

I was glad to sit beside that fire, huddled inside my cloak, even though the smoke it emitted was unnaturally active. Magically-ignited fires are always boisterously inclined, but this one appeared to be drawing an extra measure of excitement from its ancient fuel. Its flames had more blue and violet in them than red and yellow, and the smoke swirled so ingeniously that it seemed continually on the point of forming images, if not actual entities.

"Mistress," I ventured, "are these figures in the smoke not made for reading? Are they not very similar to those in the books over which you pore day and night?"

"Yes, imbecile, of course they are" she said, harshly. "It is an obvious indication that we have come to the right place. It is a welcome of sorts, I have no doubt. If we persist obstinately in our search, we shall find something greatly to our advantage." She meant, of course, her own advantage—but as I was fortunate enough to be her faithful servant, she reckoned that anything adding to her advantage must also add to mine. After that, I did not disturb her again, but I took care to study the smokeshapes myself, in the hope of improving my poor brain's capacity to identify omens and secrets and glimpse their hidden meanings.

I saw serpents and other reptilian forms in abundance, but I could not be sure that they were anything more than mere chimeras—a possibility further enhanced by the impression that so many of the serpents had wings. I sometimes dreamed in my wildest fantasies, that I too might be possessed of a Sacred Passion and the favor of a Beast-God without knowing it, because the God and the Passion had both been lost to human knowledge and inspiration with the passing of the centuries.

Alas, there was no treasure of any sort to be found in that particular ruin, even though I labored throughout the next morning moving debris from one side of an ancient floor to the other. At noon Alannah Sethyvys finally gave me permission to let the rubble alone—but that relief was only to allow me time to fetch water from a pool far below our station, and fruit from the few living trees that clung to a crevice half way around the crag.

Both of these tasks should have been simple, but there were two birds perching in the branches of one of the trees, as if they were standing sentry over their food supply. When I tried to pick the fruit they attacked me. They were more like crows than hawks, but their beaks were heavy and their talons sharp. I fought them valiantly with my knife, slashing wildly at their wings, and they concluded in the end that they were risking too much in continuing to harass me. They grudgingly withdrew, after inflicting a few nasty scratches on my face and scalp.

"A little sorcery might have helped me gather our breakfast, Mistress," I pointed out, tactfully, when I returned with my meager booty.

"Looks as woefully plain as yours will take a lot more spoiling than a few petty pecks, you miserable oaf," was her harsh reply, "and you'll have healed long before you encounter anyone who cares."

We had eaten the local fruits often enough before, when our guides were still with us. We had found them nourishing enough, though by no means sweet. The fruits of these particular trees were, however, longer and more sinuously twisted than those I had seen before, and their color was a deeper purple. To begin with, my mistress looked at them slightly askance, but she was generous enough, in view of my battle against the birds, not to complain that I ought to have found better ones. Instead, she said: "The trees must work much harder in a place like this to tempt the birds that spread their seed. Only the strongest and most prolific can cling to life amid such desolation. We shall doubtless find the fruits sweeter and more satisfying than those we have eaten before, in spite of their unprepossessing appearance."

I think she was trying to convince herself. She might even have succeeded, but I found the fruits more intoxicating than sweet. As for satisfaction....well, it is not for me to hazard guesses as to what might satisfy a scholarly sorceress and what might not.

By the time that we had completed our frugal meal the keen eyes of Alannah Sethyvys had found another likely prospect, which would have been a mere three thousand paces away had we been able to walk through the air, but seemed a great deal longer by virtue of the initial descent and the concluding climb. Again the sun was setting by the time we began the last phase of our ascent, and again it was blood-red in the face, although the light reflected from the clouds that were gathering above the plateau was burnished gold.

The second ruin was not set quite as squarely on a west-facing slope as the first, but the angle presented by the rock face only served to add an extra dimension of distortion to our monstrous shadows. The golden light reflected downwards from the clouds turned their color to a peculiar turquoise, richer and heavier than any I had ever seen before.

Fortunately—or so it seemed at the time—this ruined edifice was more extensive than the last, and a certain amount of work had been done in expanding and shaping a natural hollow in the mountain-side. There was a substantial enclosed space, which might once have been used as a storeroom, although the only relics of its former contents were a few spars that might have been broken from the sides of crates and a number of rusted hoops that might once have surrounded a barrel. There was nothing in the least resembling a clay tablet, but there were strange graffiti on the walls. They were inscribed in a script I could not decipher, which seemed to my admittedly-untutored eye not to be closely, or even distantly, akin to any language my mistress had taught me to read or copy.

Alannah Sethyvys immediately set to work examining these scrawls, and demanded that I copy them before I went in search of dead wood with which to make a fire. Much to my relief, I found more relics of manufacture—perhaps the remains of ancient chairs and tables—and did not need a magic spark to set the heap alight.

I expected the resultant fire to burn in a more orthodox fashion than the previous one, but it did not; the fuel seemed even more avid to be consumed than the wood of the dead tree, and its smoke even more enthusiastic to give birth to phantoms.

"Do we need to be anxious about these smoke-creatures, Mistress?" I asked. "If they are omens, it seems to me that they do not bode well for our future."

"And what would a cretin like you know about omens, or how to judge them?" she said, scornfully. "The only use that smoke has for a wretch like you is to make your face grimy, thus providing a mask of sorts for your ugliness. In fact, it is exactly such specters as these that have drawn us here in search of enlightenment. They are glad that we are here, because they expect us to make a discovery that will assist them to recover their lost heritage as living aspects of human beings."

"But mistress," I said, "I cannot believe that it was our own folk who built the edifice which gives us shelter now. Their lost heritage might be inimical to ours."

"Addlepate!" she cried. "What do you know of such matters?"

In Nagda I would never have dared to say anything further, but we were in a strange land where, I dared to think, familiar regulations might not apply. "Perhaps the makers of these edifices were neither humans, nor troglodytes, nor simians, Mistress," I suggested, "but some other race that has entirely vanished from the world. If it were, we could not know whether they were worshippers of Beast-Gods as well-disposed towards the various humankinds as ours are. Perhaps there were other gods in those days: gods that we could not recognize; gods, perchance, that even our gods could not recognize."

"Nincompoop!" she said—which was, I suppose, a more generous judgment than *vile blasphemer*. "Just because I have generously allowed you to serve as my eyes, even in the reading of precious texts, it does not mean that your feeble your mind could ever compare with mine. Your notions are ridiculous, befitting the fool that you are!"

I did not know whether it was Wisdom or Wrath that was using her voice, but it was obviously one of the Sacred Passions, and it was obvious that no further suggestions would be tolerated. I bowed my head submissively—and was astonished when she deigned to add a further comment of her own, which almost qualified as an explanation.

"The Wisdom of the Beast-Gods of Marakand and Arganet is, in essence, infinite and definitive," she muttered, as if she were talking to herself—and perhaps it was herself that she was trying to convince. "The gods of former eras presumably had names and forms that are now unknown to us, but there is a sense in which they must have been recognizable as the same gods. The rediscovery of the names and forms of ancient gods certainly qualifies a triumph of scholarship, and is not without its practical ramifications in the art and science of magic, even if it cannot go so far as to restore lost powers of metamorphosis. The fact is, however, that all creatures are part of One Nature and all gods are part of One Pantheon, representative of the same spectrum of Sacred Passions. The ancient secrets of metamorphosis are there to be rediscovered, if only we can find the right shadows, and read them right."

If she really was endeavoring to shore up her own faith, I suppose she might have succeeded—but she could not convince me. In my heart, I was at best a skeptic, and at worst a heretic. My interest in other passions, other gods and other worlds probably had no firmer ultimate basis that my dissatisfaction with the gods and passions of the world I knew, but it was real nevertheless.

3.

I hope I might be forgiven for inserting a philosophical interlude at this point. (I can almost hear the mocking laughter of Alannah Sethyvys as I write that line, but she is dead and I am alive, and I shall feel free to ignore the omen.)

I never dared to challenge my mistress's theological opinions, of course, and hardly dared to doubt her—but I am alone now, and certain to die, so I no longer have any fear of expressing thoughts that I would otherwise be inclined to keep secret. I dare to wonder, now, how close my mistress ever was to the Beast-Gods of Marakand and Arganet, given that she was a magician manqué, incapable of metamorphosis. I also wonder whether, as she undertook her shapereadings and pored over her ancient texts, some understandable error might have led her to mistake something else for a spectral presence echoing the image of a neglected but once-familiar god. She believed herself to be far too clever to be misled by common chimeras, and perhaps she was, but it seems to me that even the most skilful shapereader who ever lived might be led astray by uncommon chimeras. Nor is it impossible, I suspect, that the distinction between omens, specters and chimeras is not as clear as philosophical shapereaders sometimes assert

I am, of course, no certified scholar, and my mistress would doubtless think me unfit to hold an opinion on such a matter, but I read a great many books in my mistress's service, and I was never as stupid as she thought. I had wondered, even before we set out on our expedition, whether the creatures that inhabited his continent before we came might have had gods that were not Beast-Gods at all: gods that were not elements of One Nature or representatives of the Symmetrical Spectrum of the Sacred Passions, but elements and representatives of something essentially divided, shattered or contradictory. Symmetry, we are told, had its ultimate origins in Chaos, from whose raw material it was produced—and we are also told that Chaos still lurks within Symmetry, ever-ready to manifest itself as a force of decay or destruction. There might, I suppose, have been gods of Chaos once, and those gods must be as unperishable as any others, however valiantly their passions have been banished from the human heart—but there are further possibilities, which might be even more ominous.

I am, I suppose, a creature of no very great intellect—especially by comparison with a well-educated sorceress—but I like to think that I am not such a complete fool as my mistress was always glad to suggest. Thanks to her, I could not only read my own language well enough but had a smattering of others—and mine was always the kind of curiosity that seeks to tilt back the covers of forbidden books.

It goes without saying that I was always a steadfast subject of King Luthal, utterly devoted to his political causes, and it always seemed to me that someone so devoted ought to take any opportunity that presented itself to him to measure the capacity of the king's actual and potential enemies. It was for that reason, I swear, that I sometimes took the opportunity, while my mistress was otherwise engrossed, to dip into certain texts in the proscribed sections of the library of Nagda: texts that supposedly originated in the land from which the tribesmen exterminated by our colonizing ancestors had been long outcast.

I was forced to concentrate on the most harmless passages of such texts, because they were the most easily understandable; even so, I came to know a little—only a little, though perhaps far more than my entitlement—about the legends of the folk who lived in these lands before my own ancestors first learned to speak and sing. I know, for instance, that the remote ancestors of those we displaced were said to have been starfarers, and that they were said to have encountered other kinds of starfarers, who set forth from worlds circling suns so distant from our own that they do not even shine as stars in our world's night-sky. I know that emissaries of these alien races were said to have visited our world, if only briefly, although their visitations were made difficult by the fact that they were foreign to our One Nature.

Of what significance is all of this? I cannot say for sure—but I cannot help wondering whether, if worshippers of alien gods once set foot on our world, the specters of those beings might remain here too, and perhaps the phantoms of their gods. If the starfaring ancestors of the people we destroyed made of their own dead selves something that could possess smokes and vapors, why should other starfarers not have done the same? If they did, then the notion of One Nature might be a hollow myth; if so, we have no way of knowing how far the true spectrum of Sacred Passions might extend.

Because I suspected all this, I was disposed when my mistress and I took shelter in those mysterious ruins to wonder whether the race that had created them might have been closer kin to alien starfarers than to our own starfaring ancestors, and whether their gods might have been quite different from ours—far more different than the petty gods of simians, troglodytes and lycanthropes. Although we affect to despise such demihuman creatures, rightly considering them coarser and more brutal than full humans, they obviously share sufficient kinship with us to acknowledge a similar spectrum of emotions, a similar spectrum of desires, and a similar spectrum of gods. Our own Beast-Gods have their simian and troglodyte followers, even though there are no simian or troglodyte shapeshifters.

Perhaps my mistress was right, and there never was a race in this world that worshipped other gods, and perhaps no one but a cretin or an imbecile would ever try to imagine otherwise—but can we really be so certain? If there were such a race, might not the servitors who survived whatever catastrophe overwhelmed their former masters have cast magical shadows over the land, which the invasion of the Breizh could not entirely dispel? If so, is it possible that Wrath and the other Sacred Passions of the Symmetrical Spectrum were not featured among the emotions felt by those mysterious masters, or even those experienced the degenerate descendants of their servitors, who must have been slouching towards extinction long before our own forefathers learned the arts and crafts of civilization, song, and magic.

I do not believe, as the ignorant do, that common snakes and lizards are cold-blooded or devoid of passion—but I do believe that their passions must be very different from our own, perhaps echoing those of long-departed creatures of ultraserpentine or cryptosaurian kinds. It is partly to clarify in my own mind the reasons for that belief, as well as for the possible benefit of others, that I am writing this testament.

4.

There was a storm that night, when the no-longer-golden clouds turned from vapor to liquid and ice. Their water fell with an amazing violence in cold slushy sheets rather than individual raindrops and hailstones. It was as well that Alannah Sethyvys and I had a covert in which to shelter. Although its floor was liberally spattered with puddles, we kept our fire alight and our clothing dry.

I doubt that my mistress caught a wink of sleep between the thunderbolts, but I had had the benefit of a day's exhausting labor and I could not stay awake. The dazzling flashes of the lightning and the drum-rolls of the thunder became the backdrop of my dreams, which were not unduly unpleasant.

We had plenty to drink in the morning, and still had a little fruit in store, so I did not have to go to work thirsty, and the perpetual ache in my belly was not unbearable. In any case, there was less desperate sifting of stony debris to be done—although the work turned out to be no more productive than it had been before.

By the time Alannah Sethyvys had selected her third objective I felt quite well. The storm had cleared the sky of clouds and in spite of the thinness of the atmosphere the sun shone down so benignly that I was almost warm—a most unusual sensation for one born to a life in the Land of Chill.

Unfortunately, our third target was set higher on a crag than either of the others, and the way to the crag was exceedingly difficult. Before we started the ascent I was dispatched to collect more fruit, and instructed to bring back a more abundant harvest than the last time. I had to do it alone, even though my keen-sighted mistress must have known that the black birds had doubled their sentries.

To fight four huge birds with a single knife is not an easy thing to do, especially when the birds in question have long serpentine necks and talons like the fangs of asps. They raked my arms as well as my head, and tore my sleeves to shreds. One of them came within a thumb's-breath of taking out my eyes—but I drove them off in the end, and I contrived to strip the trees naked of all their remaining produce.

I got no thanks from my mistress, but again she was generous enough not to complain about the quality of the fruits I had gathered, twisted and vermiform though they were. Perhaps she really did find them sweet and satisfying; she certainly took a large enough share of my haul, consuming twice as many as were left to me.

Afterwards, as we looked up at the rocky spire looming over us, my mistress continued to assert that she had definitely seen a path, and that the way must therefore be more easily navigable than it seemed. I knew, though, what effect the kind of rain we had seen the night before must have on ledges, whether natural or artificial. Whatever winding roadway had been constructed about the crag thousands of years before had long since been reduced to a mere phantom, and I doubted that we would ever be able to reach the similarly-eroded remnant of the citadel.

Had I been alone I would certainly have turned back, declaring the task impossible, but Alannah Sethyvys was made of sterner stuff. She simply would not admit defeat. How we avoided falling to our deaths I do not know, but we survived.

When the sun reached the horizon Alannah Sethyvys and I found ourselves involved in yet another race for light, with every yard we climbed exposing another sliver of the diminishing disc. The storm had been localized, but it must have been one of many, for the air far to the west was cleaner now. The sun was orange rather than red, and the sky around it was a remarkable cerulean blue. The shadows we cast upon the rocks, therefore, should have seemed far less sinister in color, if not in shape—but that was not the case.

Our two shadows were nearly black in color, but the black still had a peculiar purple tint, which became more pronounced at the edges of each silhouette, like a violet aura. The slope was so uneven that neither shadow seemed any longer to be human; both were unnaturally elongated, especially in the limbs, and it was impossible to make out any angular joints.

If my own shadow's arms and legs resembled writhing serpents, imagine the appearance presented by the shadow cast by my taller mistress! Even had I not been too afraid to look down, I would have been fascinated by its twisting, coiling movements, and by the subtle dance of the purple aura about the black core.

It was easy—far too easy!—to imagine that the shadow was the real entity, and Alannah Sethyvys its fleshy reflection. It was easy, too, to imagine that the creature whose echo the shadow preserved might be taking advantage of a long-sought opportunity to intrude itself into the soul of a being that had power of movement in the world: a being that might carry it out of it allotted time-span at the moment of sunset, not into the soft and starry night but into the harsh dawn of the following day—and perhaps the day after that.

When the sun sank out of sight, the shadows disappeared—but I wondered whether they had merely gone into hiding once again in the vast darkness that was the shadow of the world.

This time, luck was most certainly with us. This ruin had been a grander edifice by far than the ones we had visited before. Instead of a single covert, crudely extended beneath the surface of the mountain so as to serve as a storehouse, there was a complex of rooms and corridors extending into the very heart of the crag. It was not easy to gain access thereto, because the way was all-but-blocked by fallen stones, but once we had scrambled through we came into a place that had not been subject to the fierce erosion that had washed away the road and effaced the outer structures.

There were storerooms in the cellars beneath this edifice that had been stocked by long-dead individuals which had never had the opportunity to use up their stores. Here were not merely boxes, barrels, bottles and jars—all of whose once-edible contents had decayed into mere tar—but sturdy furniture and wooden shelves, cupboards and carpets, which had not been subject to such perishing. The air was so thin, cold and dry that even clothing had survived, and scrolls of parchment too. Here, in fact, was a scholar's treasure-trove, if not a treasure-trove even for those humbler kinds of folk who like gold and gems better than books. The store-rooms even had cisterns, which collected storm-water from the slopes without and preserve it for use during periods of drought—and the cisterns were half-full.

It was everything of which my mistress had dared to dream, and I could see by the way that her eyes gleamed in the demi-obscurity how eager she was to read those parchments, which no human eye had scanned for centuries.

First of all, though, there were practicalities to attend to.

"None of this furniture is to be used as firewood, moron!" Alannah Sethyvys said to me. "There was a courtyard of sorts without, which bushes have invaded. Find firewood there and bring plenty of it in, and take care to gather any further fruit you can find in the vicinity. Take four of these pitchers and fill them with water from the cisterns, so that we can drink and bathe at will. Once we are warm and properly fed, with an abundant supply of water, we can begin work." I could tell, however, that her zeal was over-ambitious. She had had no sleep the previous night, and the long climb had exhausted her as completely as her fair share of my hard labor would have done. I knew that she would fall asleep as soon as she was warm enough, especially if she had eaten heartily.

There were fireplaces among the accumulated relics of civilized life, and I did not doubt that their chimneys would draw if only they were clean enough. They were all as wide as they were deep, and I was required to find a great deal of wood to fill the one that Alannah Sethyvys selected, but I only cheated a little. I brought as much dead wood as I could from the ancient courtyard, but the effort of scrambling over the rubble as I went back and forth was very burdensome. I brought some living wood too, but I made up the remaining deficit with the debris of broken wooden artifacts, carefully picking out bits and pieces that seemed to be of no conceivable utility or value.

If my mistress noticed my disobedience, she did not care enough to criticize me for it. All she said was: "What about the food, you miserable wretch?"

"One more trip, mistress," I said, as I filled the pitchers carefully and set them down in a row close to the bed she had improvised, with two basins and two cups close at hand. "The bushes in the yard are bare, but there are a few thorny trees higher up on the slope, which might have fruit."

I hoped that the black birds might all be asleep, but the stars seemed so close above my head and the sky was so clear that there was plenty of light enabling them to see and harass me. I thrust this way and that with my knife, so deftly that I actually managed to cripple one of the six or eight that attacked me, but when I heard its scream as it fell I realized how precarious my own position was upon the precipice. Exactly how many my attackers were I could not tell—at times they seemed to blot out the stars, although there could not have been as many as ten—but I knew that I might not be so lucky next time around, especially if the birds could raise further reinforcements.

In the end, I succeeded in gathering a further two dozen fruits, which ought to have been enough to keep us fed for at least three days while we carefully explored the ruin and examined its various treasures with all due scrupulousness. I carried the fruits triumphantly back to my mistress, not caring that my hair was matted with the drying blood from seven cuts upon my scalp. She, of course, did not care about the wounds either—and this time, she did take leave to complain that the quality of my harvests was getting poorer and poorer.

"I had high hopes of you when you were a little child, Porphyran," she told me, "but you have been a sore disappointment. My generosity in teaching you to read and write has turned you into an idle dreamer and a weakling."

5.

Despite their poor quality I had hoped to retain at least eight of the fruits that I had most recently gathered for myself, but Alannah Sethyvys was hungry, and she only left me four. Even those four made me a little drunk, but scholars are a sober breed, even when they are also sorcerers, and my mistress did not seem unduly excited.

I had contrived to light a fire without magical aid, but it had taken a strong hold by now on the hastily-assembled pyre, and the flames were compensating very generously indeed for the excitement my mistress lacked. The smoke they produced was thick and luxuriant, and it was possessed of an obvious organizing force. This time, I was perfectly certain, the shapes it produced would be more than mere impressions.

"Look, mistress!" I whispered, wonderingly, when the ultraserpentine smokeshapes began to emerge. "Those are most certainly the ghosts of things long dead—but what creatures they are!"

Alas, my mistress was already asleep. She was not quiet—indeed, she seemed to be in the grip of a fearful nightmare—but she was certainly not awake. Her eyes were closed, and she was sprawled upon the ancient carpet like a puppet deprived of its strings. I should have woken her up, even though she would have been bound to scold me, but I did not want to, not simply because she would have scolded me, but because I wanted to study the shapes by myself, to see what I might make of them without the distraction of having to look over her shoulder and cringe from her Wrathful presence. I wanted to divine whatever I could from their display.

I tried as hard as I possibly could, but the innocent hope that I might finally be able to obtain a clear image of a specter, and see exactly what kind of form it possessed, was soon dashed. There seemed to be far too many hungry souls ambitious to possess and give form to the billowing smoke; they seemed to be fighting one another fiercely for the limited resources of the fire, and no sooner had one begun to form itself with any degree of distinction that it was attacked and torn apart by others. I persisted, however, in my search for meaning, gradually becoming very eager indeed not merely to catch sight of a winged serpent or cryptosaurian reptile but to establish some sort of mental rapport with the image: to understand its significance.

It might, I suppose, have been the mere fact that the smoke was being emitted upwards into the air, drawn by a far better chimney than shapereaders' magical fires usually are, that encouraged its would-be possessors to adopt winged forms—but it is just as likely, if not more so, that the particular fire that I had built was potentially more hospitable to specters of that sort than any fire they had encountered for thousands of years. At any rate, the longer the fire burned—and I must admit that I had to keep feeding it in order to maintain its vigor, and had to disobey my mistress's orders by feeding it unspoiled items of furniture—the more intense the competition became to possess its flames.

I was convinced that there were winged serpents and tiny dragonets in vast quantities within that confusion, as well as other, more bizarre, entities that seemed to be compounded out of scaly wings and toothy mouths, without any bodies at all. Perhaps these last were mere chimeras, caused as much by the intensity of my own intoxicated vision as by the ingenuity of the smoke, but I could not help wondering whether there might be more kinds of starfarers wandering the wilderness of the firmament that the human imagination could sensibly encompass.

Tired as I was, I must have stared into the smoke above the fire for at least three hours, utterly captivated by the spectacle. It never once occurred to me turn around, even though the dutiful temperament of a loyal servant should have insisted that I ought at least to have made certain that my nightmare-afflicted mistress was safe. In all probability, I never would have turned around, had it not been for the fact that Alannah Sethyvys was seized in her sleep by a violent spasm that brought the back of her hand rudely into contact with my thigh.

As slaps go, it was nothing at all, but my reflexes had been well-trained to respond to any such blow, and I leapt to my feet automatically, turning as I did so.

When I came upright, of course, a ragged shadow cast by the firelight on the far wall of the chamber sprang up as if out of nowhere. Given that the fire was low down, with its brightest light concentrated in its hottest heart, that shadow should have been a giant, filling up the wall within its confused outline. Doubtless it would have done so, had the area in question not been occupied already by a shadow far greater, far more confused and far more possessive. Mine could not compete, and it quailed as if in terror.

Whose was that other shadow?

There is a sense, I suppose, in which the other was the shadow of Alannah Sethyvys, which had somehow drawn itself upright even though the sorceress herself was still recumbent—but I suspect that my mistress's shadow had not been entirely hers since we had made our ascent at sunset, and perhaps not for several days. Her shadow had, indeed, taken on a life of its own, not merely as her own renegade reflection but as something quite different: something left over from a time long before the arrival of the Breizh on the shore of the Sea of Sorrows. She had come here in search of the secret of ultraserpentine and cryptosaurian smokeshapes, but she had expected to find it where she had originally detected it, in smoke and the written records of previous shapereaders; in fact, she had discovered it in a different way—or perhaps it would be more accurate to say that it had discovered her, in a fashion that it had always intended, and in accordance with a plan for whose fulfillment it had long yearned.

I have no idea what forms the gods of Chaos, or the gods of ancient starfarers, might take, and I dare not take it for granted, even now, that the shadow-creature was actually the servant or reflection a god of some such sort. I do admit, though, that might have been an omen rather than a specter—but if that were so, it would not lessen my obligation to write this missive in the least. Indeed, if the thing that possessed my mistress's shadow as a warning of things to come rather than an active enemy of Symmetry, the subjects of King Luvah ought to be even more enthusiastic to receive it and act upon it. One thing of which I am certain, though, is that it was no mere chimera, no phantom of my own fevered imagination. No shapereader in the world could possibly have made an error of that magnitude.

The monster had arms of a sort, but they were like coiling serpents with gaping mouths instead of hands. It had legs, too: vast and impossibly muscular things, with vast horny toes. It had an armored crest, and a tail whose end was a bulbous mace. It also had wings, making six limbs in all—or perhaps eight, for the wings were fluttering furiously, and I could not tell whether or not their were paired on either side of the body, like the wings of dragonflies or wasps. It had a head, too, of course: a terrible, shaggy head that would have been terrifying if it had only been a silhouette, as it surely ought to have been—but the shadow was no mere silhouette limned in honest black. It was richly colored in blues and purples, rich turquoises and glaucous greens, and these continually-flowing colors displayed the features of a thousand faces upon that awful head: human faces, demihuman, reptilian, serpentine, batrachian, vulpine....and many others for which I have no ready descriptive terms.

This shadow, which already had possession of the wall where mine was suddenly cast in competition, did not react kindly to the invasion of my humble projection. It pounced upon its timid rival, with every apparent intention of obliterating it—but my shadow was still my own, or mostly mine, and its pain was more than mere nightmare to me.

I felt as if I were being raked and rent all over again by the beaks and talons of the black birds, but that my body now had a texture more like smoke than flesh, which allowed the horrid claws to pass into my substance and my soul, drawing something darker and far more precious than blood. I had tried so hard to achieve a rapport of some sort with the smokeshapes I had tried to read, never thinking for an instant that such a rapport could be anything other than an understanding, a meeting and collusion of minds. I had expected an element of passion, to be sure, but I had expected that element to be intelligibly related to the Sacred Passions embodied by the Beast-Gods and echoed in human souls.

In fact, the meeting of minds was more collision than collusion, and if any understanding at all was involved, it was all on the other side and not on mine at all. My mistress had called me "fool", or "idiot", or any one of a hundred similar insults forty or fifty times a day throughout my entire life, but I had grown so used to such invective that I had never thought to wonder what it might really feel like to be a fool—but I felt it then. As for passion—well, I had had no idea before that moment how intense passion might be, or how strange. I suppose the possession that overwhelmed me must have had something in common with Wrath, but it was certainly not akin to righteous Wrath.

I screamed, convinced that I was about to be struck dead.

6.

All of that was very strange—but the strangest thing of all was that, when the alien shadow reached into mine, ripping and devouring at one and the same time, I felt the last vestiges of my entirely natural horror and terror being utterly overwhelmed by other attitudes, which transformed them into something that I had never experienced before, nor ever thought it possible to experience.

I realized, almost immediately, that the specter had no intention of striking me dead, but was very anxious to preserve my life—or, at least, the life of my body. It had every intention of consigning my soul to oblivion, but it was avid to return to the flesh itself, and I had no doubt that, if it did, it would be a shapeshifter, capable of a tremendous metamorphosis.

I was not afraid of that possibility, though, nor even horrified by it. I was no longer capable of feeling such humdrum human emotions. Indeed, the idea of becoming a shapeshifter, and a sorcerer of great power—even though that shapeshifter would not, strictly speaking, be me at all—filled me with a strange desire.

Was that desire a passion of sorts? It was certainly not a Sacred Passion, devoted to the cause of Symmetry, but I do not know what else to call it, for the language we speak and write has no vocabulary with which to make distinctions regarding the inner darkness that lies beyond the limits of the spectrum of the Sacred Passions. In reality, though, it was *something else*: something not of our world but of worlds in the utmost depths of the starry heavens, which produced starfaring monsters long before our world was even formed.

What do I mean by that? You will, I hope, understand the difficulties that I face in trying to explain it. Writing now, of course, by daylight and in a state of relative calm, it is quite impossible for me to recapture more than the slightest echo of the sensations that flooded my mind as that strange combat progressed. I am not sure that I even have a memory of them, although there are probably voids where the relevant memories ought to be. Any such voids must be deep fissures in the fabric of my being, which only need to be extended a little way in order to make it impossible for me to *be* at all—and the situation is similar with respect to what I saw and felt.

I have read in forbidden books that the five colors we see in the rainbow—red, yellow, green, blue, and violet—are only five parts of a set of seven, and that there is more than one color that even magically-assisted eyes can only see as darkness without the assistance of esoteric sorcery. I wondered when I read it what those other colors might look like—and wondered, too, whether the impression I call "red" might be entirely different from the impression received by a demihuman or a troglodyte, which he would also call "red". Now, I am convinced that the Passions we recognize and hold sacred are not be the only ones capable of stirring a soul. I am sure that, although the sensation I call "wrath" is much the same as that called "wrath" by a goblin or a lycanthrope, and might well be an echo of the same dark god, there are other gods and other motives to violence and war. The gods worshipped by the intelligent creatures that lived in the world before humans, let alone those worshipped by ancient star-farers, were not Beast-Gods like ours—although there is, perhaps, a possibility that our own Beast-Gods are mere chimerical shadows of theirs.

I can imagine Alannah Sethyvys laughing again, but I am no longer afraid of her laughter—and I digress.

The battle of the shadows continued for a long time, and while it continued I was unable to feel any familiar kind of fear or fury. I felt so strange that I did not feel like a human being at all—and per-haps, if the battle had gone differently, I would not be one now. It was not, of course, a fight that I or my shadow could have won, but it *was* a fight from which I and my shadow could be saved.

Wood burns spitefully even at the best of times. Even the driest, deadest wood is grainy and knotted, and there is always resin in its heart whose melting causes little explosions and sparks. Wood that has been cut, shaped and polished for use in decorative furniture is often far more violent, because the efforts of artificers add to its complexity.

Sometimes, wood-fires spit out red hot splinters, with all the vi-olence of a gunshot.

Had I followed my mistress's instructions more dutifully in keeping the fire going that night, no such thing was likely to have happened, but I had been lax in my obedience.

Just as my shadow seemed to come to the point of its final de-feat, and my own soul to the point of utter annihilation, a loud ex-plosion sounded behind me. I felt a little fragment of burning wood hit the back of my own leg—but that was a trivial thing by comparison with the one that drilled three inches deep into the tender flesh of Alannah Sethyvys' left calf.

Such a shot would have awakened the most somnolent drunkard in the world, let alone a scholar and a sorceress.

Alannah Sethyvys howled in agony, and leapt to her feet cursing wildly. No matter how distant she might have been from the inmost councils of the citadels of Marakand and Arganet, she had a capacity for Wrath that many a magic-armored warrior might have envied, and it is difficult to think of anything that could have made her angrier than a red hot, needle-sharp splinter of wood piercing her to the bone.

The alien emotions that were trying to possess us were smoke and shadow still, no matter how insistent their increase might be. They had displaced the repertoire of my foolish feelings easily enough, and they had claimed the darkness of my mistress's shadow, but the flood of raw pain and wrath that coursed through her when the splinter drove into her calf was as irresistible as the sheets of cold rain that had washed the sides of the crag where we had spent the previous night.

A new shadow rose up within the two that were locked in mortal combat, and attacked the aggressor with all the fervor of the blind reflexive rage of a human sorceress. The righteous Wrath of Symmetry rose up in all its glory, to do battle with the monster from beyond the stars.

It was a fabulous battle, and while I watched it I was myself again: a poor cringing fool, crouching to one side while my mistress discharged her fury. For a little while, I actually thought that the newly-awakened shadow might win, and that Alannah Sethyvys—who was, after all, a powerful and very accomplished witch—might overcome the entity that was attempting to possess her. That illusion only lasted for a few minutes, though—five at the most.

Once I had collected myself to some degree, I realized that my mistress had woken up far too late, and that hers could be no more than a valiant rearguard action. Powerful as she was, she had been asleep too long, and her shadow had been irredeemably corrupted. Perhaps, if she too had been a shapeshifter, rather than a witch who no longer knew her hidden animal self, she might have made a better fist of it—but she was not. Alas, the alien specter had actually gained a further measure of control while disputing with mine and anticipating its return to pliable flesh; its almost-total victory over me had made it stronger.

At any rate, I saw soon enough that the new shadow, which the awakened Alannah Sethyvys had contrived to introduce into the conflict, could not endure. No matter how madly she capered, nor how loudly she swore, she could not change her shape and she could not triumph over the specter that the fire had unleashed, to which its smoke had provided a foothold in our world. The two gigantic shadows were, in the final analysis, one and the same. Both were firmly attached to Alannah Sethyvys, even if one was not, strictly speaking, hers; the only possible outcome of the battle was that the alien shadow would consume hers, and that the specter would then possess her body as it had been on the point of possessing mine when some kindly Beast-God intervened.

The splinter shot from the fire had only been an omen; it was up to me to read it, understand it and act upon it—and I did.

I drew the knife with which I had fought off the legion of black birds—whose blade glinted red in the fire's deceptive light, although I had carefully cleaned the blood away—and I hurled myself upon my mistress. She had her back to me, because she was facing the wall, and she was quite oblivious to the fact that I had moved, because she was so utterly intent on her combat. Her broad back was a perfect target, and I sank my dagger in it to the hilt, exactly where I judged the heart to be. The blade slipped neatly between the ribs. She was probably dead before she hit the floor.

The only fireshadow left on the opposite wall, for one brief second was my own—but I knew that the other would return. The specter knew its way, now; there was only one possible way of preventing it from surging back from the dancing flames into the swirling smoke, and from the multicolored smoke into the world of human beings. I had to save myself, not merely for purely selfish reasons but because I knew, now, what might happen if a creature of that sort were permitted to possess my body, my intellect and my talent for reading shapes in smoke.

Fortunately, I had set the four pitchers of water I had filled beside the bed on which my mistress had fallen asleep, in a very tidy line. I only had to stoop to pick up the first, and I discharged its contents with a single fluid motion—then I did likewise with the second, the third and the fourth.

No earthly fire could possibly have withstood such a deluge. With an almighty serpentine hiss, releasing a vast cloud of smoke that was mercifully grey and utterly chaotic, the fire was extinguished, and the world saved.

I fell down myself then, sprawling alongside the dead body of my mistress, and I lost consciousness.

7.

When I awoke the following morning, the ashes of the fire were still damp and stubbornly monochrome. The room was cold, and so was the corpse of Alannah Sethyvys. I stumbled through the dark corridors and over the rubble into the remnant of the courtyard, whose broken edge sat placidly upon the lip of the abyss. I was delighted to see the light of the rising sun brightening the sky, although the sun itself was invisible in the east, behind the mass of the crag.

The shadow of the crag extended across the pitted plateau towards the horizon, its tip disappearing at the limit of vision—but the shadow was quite black, sharply outlined and perfectly harmless. I thought that I was safe, until I saw the company of birds that had gathered in the branches of the trees that clung to the cliff-face. I counted thirty-one. Three times I had beaten a lesser number back— but in so doing, I had advertised myself as a dangerous enemy, which had to be defeated.

The birds only watched me balefully while I was content to draw great unsatisfying draughts of cold, thin air into my lungs—but they were waiting, and I knew that they would not tolerate any approach. I realized then that they were not the only ones who had marked me. No matter where I was when sunset came again—even if I huddled in the darkness in the heart of the mountain, fully determined to make do without a fire—I knew that the shadows of the distant past would consider me their legitimate quarry: the means of the only re-entry into the world that they could possibly contrive.

I realized, in fact, that there was no way out of my predicament, and no way back to civilization. Alannah Sethyvys had brought me too far from the edge of the plateau, and I could not get back alone without a much better supply of food than the birds would every permit me to gather.

That is my situation as I write. Even if I could withstand the pangs of hunger, I could not go out into the open by day without casting the kind of shadow that would rise up against me and dispossess me of my fear, my anger and my soul. Even by night, if the moon and stars were shining, I would be in dire danger, and not merely from the bitter cold that precedes the dawn.

Perhaps, if I had ever been as close as Alannah Sethyvys to the authentic and righteous Wrath of the spectrum of Sacred Passions, I might be able to arm myself against the specter's assault, but I was ignobly born and am still something of a fool, in spite of all my ill-gotten learning. I do not have it in me to surrender myself entirely to constructive rage, courage, or obstinacy—or, indeed, any other gift of the Beast-Gods. I received more than my due when the omen from the fire told me what I had to do to hold back the forces of darkness from the greater world; the Beast-Gods never intended me to save my own worthless life.

And that is why I am writing this account of my adventure.

There are plenty of bottles here, and I have the means to seal one securely. Even my poor eyes can make out the course of a stream which runs from the base of the crag, and there is water seeping into it still from the storm that burst over my head the night before last. I know that I can get down to the bottom of the crag, although I am not entirely sure that I could get up again, if I wanted to.

There might, I suppose, be ordinary treasures here, but if there are, the only implication of their presence is that this place is a potential trap for humble folk as well as ambitious scholars. I believe that it *is* a trap, whether deliberately set or not, and that is why I am honor bound to issue this warning.

Do not send anyone in search of Alannah Sethyvys, or to follow the rumor that she was commissioned to investigate.

Stay away from this place, because it is not fit for any beings of our kind, whichever gods they serve and whichever Sacred Passions they possess.

That is, I suppose, all I need or ought to say—but mine is the kind of curiosity that tilts back the covers of forbidden books, and there is one more dire thought of which I cannot rid myself.

Alannah Sethyvys was one of a host of sorcerers whose work it is to investigate the meanings of smokeshapes, desperate to discover what omens they might bring regarding the possibilities of the future and the course of the great war between Symmetry and Chaos. I, who was only her servant, have little or no right to express an opinion on such matters, but in view of what I have lately seen and felt I cannot help but wonder whether there is less difference than we might think between echoes of the distant past and forebodings of the future.

Even after its emergence from Chaos, the universe of stars and the little sliver of Symmetry that our world constitutes were once the dominion of creatures so unlike ourselves that perhaps our very gods are merely shadows of theirs. No one can know whether ancient starfarers really did visit our world, or why, if they did, neither they nor their protégés are any longer here, but there is one thing of which we can be perfectly certain: there will eventually come a day when our own tenure here is done, and beings of yet another kind will call the world their own. Perhaps that is what the shapes in the smoke of our fires are really trying to tell us.

If so, all the produce of divine Wrath and justice that we believe we can read therein might be no more than froth and foam upon the irresistible tidal wave of time.

RECONSTRUCTION

He ran up the stairs as soon as he heard the scream, taking them two at a time. He grabbed the door-handle but it was locked. She must have seen it turn because he heard her let out another yell for help. He stood back and hit the door with his heel, just above the lock. The wood splintered around the lock and it only needed a second kick to hurl the door open.

The girl was up against the wall. She was in a bad way—absolutely hysterical. *Who wouldn't be*, he thought, *with that thing waving a knife at her?* It *was* just a *thing*, not a person; he knew full well that whatever was human had been blotted out by the accident and by whatever the doctors had done to bring it back to life.

"Get back!" he said—but it didn't take a blind bit of notice. He had to draw the gun. He had no choice.

He knew that he had hit it with the first shot, but it didn't fall. It didn't seem to have felt the impact. The knife was still in its hand, and it was still coming at him. He had to shoot twice more.

The third shot finally knocked it back, and it crumpled up, writhing like some great ugly insect. When he was sure it was down for good he went to the girl and tried to calm her down.

"Looks like I was just in time," he said.

* * * * * * *

She backed up against the wall, but he just followed her. His eyes were funny—she could see the whites all around the irises. He was biting his lip, and he seemed to be in pain. She felt as if she were stuck to the wall, as if she were being sucked into the surface by the force of her fear. She knew that she ought to lash out with her feet but she couldn't do it. She couldn't even scream.

This isn't happening, she told herself. *No matter what they did, he can't be alive. He can't be.*

She heard a bang as something hit the door, and the living dead man abruptly turned away, startled and anguished. She couldn't tell whether there was any intelligence at all in his movements, or whether it was all just stimulus and response, like an animal. Now that his uncanny eyes were no longer staring into hers she was able to turn her own head.

The door gave way at the second attempt and the man with the gun came in. He seemed to be terrified even before he caught sight of the man with the knife, and he was already raising the gun to fire. The man who had been dead put up his arms as if he thought he could ward off bullets with his bare arms, and the light flashed on the blade of the kitchen-knife he'd picked up downstairs. He backed away, but the man with the gun followed him, firing three times.

As soon as she saw the scarred man fall the paralysis seemed to drain out of her. She relaxed, and suddenly she found herself leaning against the wall for support. She would have fallen over if the man with the gun hadn't caught her by the shoulders. His eyes were funny—she could see the whites all around the irises. He looked almost as crazy as the man he'd shot.

"Thank God!" she said. "You were just in time."

* * * * * * *

The girl pressed her body back against the wall, as if she were trying to burrow into it. He opened his mouth to tell her not to be afraid, but no words would come out. He couldn't move properly—his legs wouldn't respond, although he'd managed to turn the key with the fingers of his left hand. He'd had to do that, to keep the pursuers out while he had a chance to explain—if only he *could* explain.

There was a loud bang as something hit the door. He turned towards it fearfully. At the second attempt the lock gave way and the door flew open. The man who came through it was already firing his pistol. He put up his hands in what was meant to be a placatory gesture but it was already too late. He felt the impact as first bullet hit him, but there was no pain—no pain at all. He tried to say "No!" but even that was beyond his power. Then he felt the second bullet. Still there was no pain, but he was knocked off balance, and his limbs could no longer support him. After he fell, the gunman fired a third time, into his supine body.

What's the point? he thought. *Aren't I dead already?*

The man with the gun seemed to be paralyzed; he didn't move for some time. The girl was still slumped against the wall.

"It was self-defense," said the man with the gun, finally. "You saw it. It was self-defense."

"What does it matter?" said the girl, breathlessly. "He—it—was dead anyway."

He knew that it was true. He was dead, and no longer had the least control over his limbs. Somehow, though, his consciousness simply would not dissolve, and could not be displaced.

Had there been a transcendental light, he would have gone towards it, as proverbial wisdom advised—but there wasn't even darkness.

THE RETURN OF THE DJINN

1.

Edmond Kerval watched enviously as his Arab companion wound the reins of his horse round his saddle-horn, stiffened his legs, turned the upper part of his body through half a circle and drew back his bowstring. Ahmad Meljul took aim as carefully as was possible, given that his horse was traveling at full gallop, and fired. As soon the arrow was released, the bowman turned back to take up the reins and regain full control of his mount.

It was left to Kerval, looking back over his shoulder, to observe that the missile had flown straight into the breast of one of the pursuing camel-riders. "One down!" he cried, exultantly—and then, raising a fist into the air, he said: "And they've had enough! They're not prepared to lose any more like that!" He spoke in the Latin-based patois that still remained the common tongue of the North African trade caravans, more than three centuries after the fall of Rome; it was nowadays the language in which Kerval framed his private thoughts, so long had it been since he had last had occasion to speak his native Breton tongue.

The remaining Tuaregs were bringing their camels gradually to a halt, and their no-less-mysterious companions immediately followed their example. The two fleeing riders reined in without further delay, knowing that they had to preserve the strength of their animals. Their horses gladly slowed to a canter, and then to a walk.

When the Arab finally consented to speak, he did not echo Kerval's optimism. "The Veiled Ones never give up—nor do their new companions, if rumor can be trusted. They've decided to play a long game. It's a wise move—loaded camels can't outrun horses as lightly loaded as ours over a short distance, and there's no necessity for camel-riders to sprint when they can easily out-stay their quarry. If they don't lose our trail, they're sure to catch up eventually, and they know it. All they have to do is to wait for our mounts to collapse from exhaustion and want of water. We'll be easy prey then." Meljul spoke the caravan patois with the utmost fluency, having spent far longer as a mercantile mercenary than Kerval, but he always spoke it in a measured manner; having far more opportunities than Kerval to speak his native Arabic, he presumably still couched his own thoughts in that language.

The ill-assorted band that had been chasing the two companions since dawn was by no means large; it had numbered no more than eight Tuaregs to start with—two of whom had now been killed or disabled by Meljul's arrows—and half a dozen of their sinister companions, who did not wear the distinguishing purple veil of the desert-dwelling tribesmen but were no less enigmatic. Kerval had not seen one of them at close range, but he knew that the faces he had glimpsed within their white cowls had the appearance of death's-heads—for which reason he and Meljul had dubbed them "skull-faces". They might have been wearing masks, but he feared that they were not. Whoever or whatever they were, though, he and his Arab companion would be overwhelmed quickly enough if they had to fight on foot.

A long career working with the trade caravans seemed to have given Meljul a useful education in many kinds of fighting, and the training Edmond Kerval had received as a youth in his distant homeland had made him unmatchable in swordsmanship by any scimitar-wilding desert tribesman, but the Breton knew that there was no way that the two men would be given the chance to defend themselves in their own chosen fashion. This was now a careful war of attrition, in which their enemies would take full advantage of the most powerful enemy of them all: the desert.

"I can't understand why they ever thought it worth their while to chase us," Kerval said, with a sigh. "If we possessed anything worth stealing, apart from our weapons, we'd hardly be deep in this inhospitable land following crazy rumors of treasure."

"I doubt that it's mere robbery they have in mind," Meljul said, dully.

"What then? They can't be planning to capture us in order to sell us into slavery—they must suspect that we'll fight to the death if we have to. The potential reward isn't worth the risk."

"They might make the calculation differently," Meljul told him, grimly. He said no more, but Kerval thought that he could follow the Arab's train of reasoning. The Tuaregs might be assuming that they would be able to take their two victims easily enough once thirst had driven them crazy—and if that really was what they had in mind, they probably did not have any ordinary slave-market in mind. The rumors circulating in the souks along the trade-route were much more prolific in Arabic than patois, so Meljul must be much more familiar with them than Kerval was, but the Breton had picked up the gist of the darker tales; the fact that the skull-faces were with the Tuaregs lent a new plausibility to the most incredible among them.

Kerval found himself strangely reluctant to ask the other man whether his deductions were correct. "It's not as if we might be thought to be infringing any territorial rights," he complained, obliquely. "This desert is no longer capable of supporting any kind of life. The last supposed oasis we found had barely enough water to fill a cup, and we had to dig for that; no nomad tribe would attempt to water its herds there."

"It's not a matter of territorial rights, any more than it's a matter of mere theft," Meljul observed. "Bretons might think in those terms, but the Tuaregs don't."

Again, Kerval thought he knew that the other man meant. Most nomads—even the majority of the desert Bedouin—were herdsmen who moved from oasis to oasis in quest of grazing for their livestock, and who were, therefore, inclined to think of the oases and their bounty as "theirs", but the Tuaregs were different. The Tuaregs were predators pure and simple, who lived off the herds of others. They were outcasts of a sort, forced into the margins of the greater society of the Bedouin, and the wilderness made a useful refuge from which to mount their raids. Even so, Kerval was surprised to have found them this far south in the most desolate of desert regions, and quite prepared to head even further southwards in pursuit of a couple of coastal strays. In all probability, the Tuaregs would never have spotted Kerval and Meljul in the first place if they had not been heading this way for some other reason. Whatever purpose the Tuaregs had had before they stumbled across the horsemen, however, they seemed to have a new one now: to hunt the horsemen down.

"We might be able to double back behind them, and then do our best to pick them off one by one when they make camp," Kerval said. He felt slightly uncomfortable proposing a plan that would require far more of the bowman's skills than of his own, but he could see no other possibility of turning things around.

"Impossible," was Meljul's brutal judgment.

"What can we do, then?" Kerval asked, his voice taut.

"We have no choice but to go on," the Arab said, "and hope that we can find a way to give them the slip before our mounts die on us." He plainly did not believe that they were likely to succeed in that, either—but at least it did not qualify as a blatant impossibility.

Kerval looked at the terrain that lay before them, and knew exactly why his companion was so pessimistic. The deserts of Araby did not seem so bad when one was traveling with a caravan, from oasis to oasis, but he and Meljul were a long way south of the trade route now. This region of the wilderness must have been fertile once, because the stumps of dead trees could sometimes be found, and the outlines of stone foundations that must once have supported sizeable buildings, but its fertility had obviously gone into a steep and irreparable decline centuries before; there was only sand and rock in view at present. The sand was gathered by the wind into continually-shifting dunes, which limited the range of his vision to a few hundred paces. Although noon was long past the sand was very hot as well as yielding, and it was far from being an ideal surface for steel-shod horses. Kerval and Meljul had put leather socks over the hooves of their mounts, but that precaution had not been enough to save them from distress.

Kerval raised his water-bottle and shook it. There was hardly enough liquid to rattle, and he put it down again even though his throat was parched. "If we don't find water by nightfall," he observed, grimly, "We'll be traveling on foot tomorrow. If we don't find water before tomorrow's sunset, it might be a mercy were the

Tuaregs to catch up with us sooner rather than later, and give us the chance to sell our lives dearly in honest combat. All we can do, though, is keep going forward hopefully. The one thing to be said for these dunes is that there always seems to be high ground ahead, and no way of knowing what might be behind it."

"More dunes," the Arab muttered. Kerval guessed that the odds were a hundred to one in favor of that judgment, and perhaps a thousand to one—but to his surprise, Ahmad Meljul modified it almost immediately. "There was some sort of road here once, though," the Arab added, pensively.

"I can see no sign of it," Kerval admitted.

"You're not desert-bred," Meljul reminded him, unnecessarily. "It must be far older than any I've seen before, but it's definitely a road."

"Your desert-bred Tuaregs will presumably see it as easily as you do," Kerval said. "Perhaps we should get off it."

"No," his companion said, curtly. "We won't lose anything by following it, at least for a while. The buried surface offers the horses better purchase than they'd find on deep sand. The road must have led somewhere once; if there's any water to be found, it'll probably take us there."

"It must lead to the city!" Kerval exclaimed, feeling a sudden surge of exultation. "Étienne Marin was telling the truth! It might lead us to a fortune."

"It's infinitely more likely to lead us to damnation," was Ahmad Meljul's harsh verdict. "Not that it matters. There comes a time in every man's life when all roads lead to damnation."

Kerval was already familiar with Ahmad Meljul's fatalistic streak. He knew, too, that his companion had never had the slightest faith in his treasure-hunting project, and that the discovery of an all-but-obliterated road would be insufficient to ignite the slightest spark of enthusiasm for it. The Breton could hardly blame his friend, for he had almost lost all faith in the tale himself, having made a new appraisal in the informant who had told him the tale and sent him forth on this mad expedition. As a boy, he had thought Étienne Marin a fine fellow, and a hero of sorts; having sought his own fortune in the lands of North Africa, however, he knew now that his cousin had probably been a commonplace liar, trying to make his own failure seem less abysmal than it was.

From a rational viewpoint, Kerval could find little comfort himself in the news that there had once been a road here that only a desert-bred Arab could now detect—but he was still prepared to nurse the last flickering flame of hope that there might be treasures of a sort to be found in this once-inhabited realm. *The fact is,* he thought, *that we might as well cling to the hope that Marin was right, given that we've so little else to offer us any hope at all.*

Kerval was a native of Léonais—and, more specifically, of the port of Is, whose noblemen and commoners alike were exceedingly proud of their ancient naval traditions, and made great heroes of their tradesmen and privateers. Although they were far too proud of being Bretons to claim, as the Basques of southern Aquitania were wont to do, that they were descended from the civilized inhabitants of a lost continent on the far side of the Great Ocean, the old mariners of Brest sometimes claimed to have seen the land in question, and often told tales of the fabulous treasures possessed by the dwellers in its vast jungles.

Perhaps I should have set off westwards instead of coming south when I left to seek my fortune, Kerval thought. *I'd be very glad to trade this desert for a jungle, even if demons and the dead were not rumored to have returned in force to this pestilential land, in order to make compacts with the worst of the living.*

Mindful of the bad example set by their neighbors, the Picards and Normans—whose pirate-descended families were perennially engaged in feuds and conspiracies—the Breton nobility often found it conducive to political stability to put their younger sons in charge of ships that were commissioned to undertake expeditions to distant and dangerous parts of the world, so Kerval really might have joined a ship whose captain was crazy enough to risk the perils of the Great Ocean. Attempting to be sensible, though, he had taken a more conventional choice, joining a two-master that plied the well-worn trade-routes along the African coast of the Mediterranean. Alas, well-worn trade-routes also attacked pirates like dung-flies, and he had been lucky to escape when the vessel was raided and sunk.

Once on land, the reputation Bretons had for reliability and swordsmanship had gained him employment as a caravan mercenary, but the pay had been too poor and the life-expectancy too low to tempt him to make a career of it, so he had been yearning to turn treasure-seeker for some time before the new friend whose acquaintance he had made in the mercenary trade, and whose friendship he had quickly cultivated, had reacted a little too fiercely against the overweening arrogance and unreasonable demands of one of his employers. Even killing a caravan-master would have been enough to win them both the fatal title of outlaw—Kerval being considered guilty by association—but killing a merchant had been enough to put a tempting price on their heads, and had made it necessary to quit the region entirely.

Kerval had always known, of course, that of every hundred scions of Breton families who set out to make their fortunes in the great wide world, only one was likely to return rich, while fifty never returned at all, but those odds had somehow seemed far better in the souks of Tunis and the quays of Brest than they did now that he was lost in the desert. He would have gladly settled, at the moment, for being one of the forty-nine out of that hundred who arrived home in rags, with nothing to show for their adventures but tales of treasures *almost* captured and battles *almost* won. Such tales were usually discounted as pathetic excuses, but when one of Kerval's own cousins, whom he had been careless enough to admire, had assured him that no one but loyal Edmond should have the tale of what had *really* happened to the crew of his lost ship, Kerval had been far too eager to believe him…and when he had remembered the tale as he and Meljul fled Tunis, he had fallen prey to an enthusiasm that far more nostalgia in it than intelligence.

"I've heard some talk of a dreadful Land of the Dead that lies on the edge of the desert," Kerval said to his fellow rider, tentatively, when the silence became unbearable again, "but I had thought it a mere nightmare, based on misremembered accounts of Egypt's ancient past, and something that belonged, in any case, to the remote past. Do you really think that the skull-faces might have come from some such land?"

"I don't know what to think," Meljul replied, tersely.

"They're certainly not mummies escaped from some Egyptian tomb," Kerval went on, uncomfortably aware of the silliness of the suggestion. If their faces really are representative of their entire bodies, they're more like the animated skeletons I've seen painted on Church walls in my homeland, brandishing the scythes that bring in the human harvest, or leading the Dance of the Dead to the Other World."

"I'd rather they didn't come close enough for us to get a clearer sight," Meljul replied.

"Agreed," said Kerval. "I'd appreciate the advice of an Arabic speaker, though, as to the nature of the legendary Land of the Dead, just in case the reports of its recent renewal have some basis in fact. Even if it's only a matter of a few bandit tribesmen adopting masks in preference to veils, I'd like to know what effect they're trying to achieve."

"If that's what it is," Meljul told him, "what they're trying to do is persuade more civilized folk that the djinn are returning, after a thousand years in bondage, and that an age of chaos is about to descend upon North Africa—and Europe too."

Kerval did not like the sound of that at all, although he had only the vaguest notion of what Meljul was talking about. "I thought your Arab djinn were what we in Christendom call demons," he said. "I had no idea that they had ever been put away."

"Legend has it that they gave mankind a great deal more trouble in the distant past," Meljul told him, "until the great mage-king Suleiman was given a special dispensation by Allah to punish them for their depredations. As the tales tell it, Suleiman was given a sign with which to bind them. Some he sealed in brass bottles, which were hurled into the sea; others he chained up underground, in caverns hollowed out by the waters that were more abundant in those days. The seal was guaranteed for a thousand years, some say—but that means little more, in legendary parlance, than 'a long time.' In any case, some astrologers, who claim to be inheritors of long tradition, and other proclaimers of woe—of which the souks never have and shortage—have recently claimed that the thousand years are due to elapse in the present generation, and that the seals are breaking of their own accord. Others say that a handful of seals have recently been broken by human carelessness—by fisherman who drew brass bottles from the sea, or treasure-seekers delving in the caverns—and that the djinn thus freed are swiftly finding ways to liberate their kin. In either case, the once-imprisoned djinn are said to be exceedingly annoyed with humankind in general, and the descendants of Suleiman in particular—and those who believe, or pretend to believe, in their return say that they are planning a monumental vengeance, which will extend far beyond death for its luckless victims."

The Arab's tone had shifted markedly as he spoke, in his curiously painstaking fashion. In the beginning, he had tried to feign amusement, as befitted someone commenting on an imposture by ingenious bandits, but as his account had progressed, the authority of the tales had asserted itself in spite of his unbelief, and his voice had become wholly earnest. Kerval suspected that there was a deeply superstitious man lurking beneath his friend's cynical surface…as there probably was, he had to confess, beneath his own. "Might it have been djinn, then," the Breton asked, "that we saw riding with the Tuaregs?"

"The djinn are far too proud to do that," Meljul told him, evidently trying to regain a jesting tone, "but if they really have begun reanimating the dead for use as slaves and instruments of vengeance, it's possible that the Tuaregs are riding with their own lost relatives. If that's the case, the man I shot with my bow a little while ago might be back in the saddle very soon, albeit a little leaner and lacking in warm wet blood."

"Perhaps you should have aimed at the camel," Kerval said, wishing that he had the heart to make an honest joke of it, since his companion plainly did not. He blinked furiously, trying to moisten his eyes. The sun was lower in the sky now, but that only made it more difficult for his eyes to avoid, no matter how far he tilted the brim of his hat sideways; he envied Meljul his more capacious headdress.

"If men can be reanimated, so can animals," Meljul told him, in a voice that had flattened considerably, squeezing out the last remaining vestiges of skepticism as well as optimism. "The powers of djinn are doubtless not unlimited, and whatever they do must bear some cost, but if they really are returning in force…well, I suppose we must hope, if our fate is to be conscripts in another mercenary army than the one we recently left behind, that there is some provision, however small, for its soldiers to share in its triumphs and its spoils."

2.

Given the circumstances, Ahmad Meljul had not been at all worried, at first, as to the exact direction he ought to take in fleeing the place where he had killed the merchant; his one and only priority had been to get away. He had felt far more guilty about the fact that he had dragged his new friend into his own self-made catastrophe than about killing the filthy swine whose blood he had spilled—and that had caused him to extend more sympathy than he would otherwise have done to the Breton's foolish desire to go treasure-hunting.

There had seemed little alternative but to go southwards, since the caravan-route extended eastwards and eastwards, and the ports to the north were also merchant territory—and little alternative too, to coming much further south that he had ever been before. The sheer insanity of the imaginary destination that his friend had in mind had seemed entirely appropriate to the insanity of his own action, and the plight that he was now in. He had not given much thought, in the beginning, to the rumors that had been circulating in the souks regarding dark happenings in the south, and any thought that had crossed his mind had accounted them a fortunate circumstance, likely to deter pursuit. When he had actually caught sight of the men without faces who were keeping company with the Tuaregs, though, Meljul had been forced to review his situation. As he and the Breton made their way deeper and deeper into what now seemed like dire peril, he had become exceedingly thoughtful.

It did not help his mood that the Breton had become irritatingly talkative. That tendency had seemed attractive when they first met, because Meljul did not find it easy to talk to other men, and it was good to have a friend who gladly bore the strain of maintaining their relationship, but now it only served as a provocation stirring up dark and monstrous fears.

"Perhaps we should have sold our horses and bought camels," Kerval opined, wearily, as their exhausted mounts crested yet another rise, only to display more dunes laid out before them, as far as the eye could see. "If we can somehow contrive to get the better of the Tuaregs and their skeletal allies, though, we might still effect a useful exchange."

"I might have been reduced to guarding caravans," Meljul replied, attempting to be proud and scornful but only succeeding in being dully whimsical, "but my family is as highly-esteemed in my own country as yours apparently is in Léonais. We aristocrats of Araby are horsemen through and through; to us, camels—like donkeys—are mere beasts of burden. Tuaregs ride them by choice, but it would require the direst necessity to make me do likewise."

Kerval shrugged his shoulders, but offered no apology. Privately, Meljul supposed, the Breton probably thought that the least of the noble families of his much-vaunted Is must be a match for the best in Araby, but he would not dream of saying so, at least in the language of the caravans.

Meljul looked back at the way they had come, pensively. Earlier in the day there had been a wind blowing, which had held out the hope that their tracks in the soft sand might be obliterated, but the dusk through which they were now riding was utterly still and the route they had followed could hardly have been marked more clearly. It could not be helped. There was nothing to do but continue going forward, in the hope of finding harder ground. If they could not find some opportunity to put their enemies off the scent, they would have to keep moving until their mounts could move no more. After that, he and the Breton would be forced to continue on foot, until they, in their turn, became incapable of moving on.

Meljul knew that the foreigner would inevitably be the first of the two men to fall. If and when that happened, the sensible thing for him to do would be to press on without him, glad of the possibility that the Breton might cause his pursuers enough delay, even while dying, to give him a better chance of slipping away.

But how can I do that? the Arab thought, *when it is entirely my fault that he is out here, lost in this alien land? He is my responsibility now. At least he will never have the opportunity to pass on his crazy tale of treasure to some other wide-eyed cousin in his precious Is, who will know no better than he did whether or not to take it seriously. What could I have been thinking, to indulge his fantasy, when I know so much better than he does what such silly stories are worth? Buried cities older than the desert sands! Temples raised to evil gods when the fabled Land of the Dead not only existed, but was still a Land Shared with the Living! Horned idols with enormous gems mounted in their foreheads! How could he ever have been so gullible? How could I ever have let him remain so gullible, when I became his friend? And yet...we are, indeed, following a road of sorts, which must lead somewhere, as well as to damnation.*

Kerval's raw voice cut into his reverie: "Look there, Ahmad!"

For a moment, Meljul's carefully-balanced cynicism tipped over, releasing a flood of delirious hope—but then he saw that the Breton was pointing up into the sky, where half a dozen vultures were patiently circling. His momentary optimism faded into bitterness—but then he revived it, telling himself that it might, after all, be a good omen rather than an evil one.

Kerval's reaction had evidently moved in the opposite direction, once he realized what the birds were. "Have they come for us already?" the Breton groaned. "Is the odor of death already upon us?"

"Not yet," Meljul said, trying to moisten his mouth so that his voice would not croak. "They must have more urgent work to do. There's something up ahead that is not quite dead."

"And if we get there first," Kerval said, attempting to feign casual sarcasm, "we can hold the birds at bay and claim the prize for ourselves!"

It was not such a stupid hope as the Breton seemed to imagine. "Perhaps we can," Meljul said, softly, urging his horse to one last effort. Kerval copied him, although neither mount made any evident response.

The sun's rim had vanished now, although its rays, slanting from beyond the horizon, still tinted the sky-borne dust that caravan-drivers called the Harmattan, staining the purple sky with blood red. Meljul knew that the twilight would not last long. His horse was all-but-finished, even though it was drawing slightly ahead of Kerval's in response to his coaxing. There was no danger, as yet, that Kerval would be left far behind—but Meljul was not about to slow down until his sense of obligation forced him to do so.

The dunes were smaller and steeper hereabouts than they were behind, and the low ground between them was conspicuously stonier. The evidence of the long-disused road was becoming increasingly clear, even though its course was no longer running straight. It still made good sense for Meljul to follow the meandering course of the ancient path, even though he could hardly see twenty paces in front or behind in the darkening dusk, and would soon be unable to see anything at all.

Ten minutes passed before they came in sight of the vultures' quarry. When they did, Meljul's first reaction was to groan in disappointment. He had been hoping, albeit desperately, to find another human traveler. Had he given his fantasy full rein, it might even have been a pretty woman, for preference, who had fainted from the heat even though she still had a full water-bottle—or, better still, a barrel—in the luggage borne by her team of sturdy and patient pack-horses. In fact, it was only a camel: a beast exactly like those the Tuaregs rode. It carried no saddle or harness, but it had almost certainly escaped from domestication; wild camels had long been extinct in the region. It might, in fact, have belonged to one of the Tuaregs that he had shot that morning, which had contrived to shed its load and gallop off rather than being kept as a pack-carrier by its former owner's cousins, and had contrived to overtake their horses by following a slightly different route.

At any rate, the animal was lying down rather than squatting, presumably fatally stricken by thirst and exhaustion. Its eyes were open, and they moved to fix upon Meljul as the Arab rode towards it—but the creature seemed incapable of any movement, save for a reflexive spasm in one of its hind legs.

Trying to reignite his optimism, Meljul told himself that the animal was meat, and a very lucky find—but meat was not what he needed most. It was water that he needed, and desperately. He wondered, briefly, whether his horse might be persuaded to drink a camel's blood, and whether the animal would get any benefit out of it if it could be so persuaded. Having failed to convince himself in respect of the horse, he wondered if he could persuade himself to drink a camel's blood, and whether he would get any benefit from it if he could. He was not surprised to observe that Edmond Kerval seemed even less excited by the discovery than he was.

"Is this really worth fighting the vultures for?" Kerval asked.

Meljul was certain that it was—and could not help wondering whether there might yet be a greater advantage to be gained. "Camels have good noses," he retorted, thoughtfully.

Kerval, looking down at the animal's ugly and flaccid snout with evident distaste, was evidently thinking that *good* did not mean *handsome*.

"Look at its tracks, Edmond!" Meljul instructed his companion. "Its path has converged with ours. I can't be sure where it started from, although I can probably claim credit for setting it free, but the important thing is that it surely would not have come this way if there were a better way to go. If there's water anywhere nearby, this is the signpost that will lead us to it."

"If it's more than a few hundred paces off, it might as well be on the other side of the world," Kerval said, glumly.

Meljul dismounted, searching the terrain with his eyes. "It's not!" he said, almost immediately. "It's right here—but the poor creature couldn't get to it. It's a well, my friend, and a covered well at that! That's why the road suddenly became so round-about—it was making a detour to this spot. There was a dwelling here once—can't you see the remains of a stone wall, over there?"

Kerval did not even look in that direction. The sole focus of his attention, now, was the well; the mere word on Meljul's lips had evidently revived his hopes.

Meljul knew from awful experience that a well did not always mean water—not, at any rate, without the trouble of digging down into the soil—but a possibility was a possibility. By the time the Breton had drawn level with his own horse and the other rider had dismounted, Meljul was already using his booted feet to brush the sand away from a rounded stone, whose emergent shape declared clearly enough that it was no mere boulder. It was a sculpted cap-stone. "Help me!" the Arab demanded of his friend.

Kerval was not slow to oblige.

The capstone was heavy, but its weight had been carefully judged so that a lone man would be able to slide it away in case of dire necessity, and the two of them shifted it without undue difficulty.

Night had fallen now, but they would not have been able to see far into the pit even in broad daylight. Meljul picked up a pebble, no bigger than a knucklebone, and dropped it into the black pit. The splash was somewhat delayed, but clearly audible and satisfyingly sonorous; it promised reasonable depth. "We have a rope, if not a bucket," the Arab said, exultantly. "One of us can let the other down, with a rope around his waist and a bottle in each hand. It might take four or five descents, but we should be able to bring up enough to put new life into the horses. It will be exceedingly tiresome, but well worth the trouble."

"I'm lighter than you are," Kerval pointed out, "and you have the stronger arms—but the water's a fair way down. Is the rope long enough, and will it take the strain?"

"There's only one way to find out," Meljul told him, already rummaging in his saddle-bag for the rope, and raising no objection to the suggestion that Kerval should make the descent while he did the donkey-work.

Kerval took off his belt, including his sheathed sword and his pouch, and passed them to his companion, saying: "These are all my remaining worldly possessions, my friend—everything that I possess, at present, is attached to this belt. Look after it, I beg you."

Meljul nodded reluctantly, slightly uneasy about having to take on even more responsibility for the foreigner's life and fortune, but he had no alternative but to accept it. "You'll be back in three minutes," he muttered.

Unfortunately, it only required two minutes to ascertain that the rope was not long enough to the plumb the well, and that Meljul would be unable to bear Kerval's weight for much longer than that, even though the Breton had disemburdened himself of his sword and other possessions.

"Lower!" said the Breton's voice, echoing strangely as it resounded from the pitch-dark depths. "Keep lowering me down!"

"I can't!" Meljul told him. "There's no more rope to unwind—I'll have to pull you up again…if I can."

"All right," the Breton conceded. "We'll extend it somehow—four or five feet ought to do it."

Ahmad Meljul began to haul on the rope, hoping desperately that he still had strength enough to bring the other man back to the rim. He knew that he had to do that, if he could—but he did not have the opportunity to find out whether he could. Almost as soon as his the strain in his muscles turned to pain, the rope broke and the burden at its far end was suddenly no longer there.

Meljul fell backwards, landing painfully on the base of his spine.

3.

As Edmond Kerval made the judgment that another four or five feet of cord might be necessary to allow him to reach the water in the well, he braced himself as best he could against the walls of the shaft, trying to minimize the strain on the rope and his friend's arms. It was to no avail; a worn section of the rope snapped somewhere in the loop securing it about his torso, and he fell out of the noose.

He could not find a handhold or a foothold in the wall, and scrabbling after them only served to bloody his hands. His natural optimism told him that he could not have far to fall, though, and that he probably would not hurt himself, because he was falling into deep water. He was entirely right, although the second part of his conviction turned out to be slightly better grounded than the first.

As things turned out, Kerval fell less than twice his own height, but he ripped his fingernails badly trying to slow the precipitate descent. When he hit the water, though, the impact seemed adequately cushioned, and he did not strike the bottom with a rude shock. He was astonished to find that the water was cold—although the more surprising thing, had he only had time to consider the matter, was that it was far from still. Even before he hit the water, the circle of light at the well-mouth seemed to have shrunk alarmingly; once he was immersed he was in total darkness—and by the time he had struggled back to the surface, the current had carried him away.

He was not at all disappointed to be wet, of course, nor to be filling his mouth with water as he fought for balance, but he knew that he was in dire danger. At any moment the flow might dash him against a rock or carry him into a bottleneck where he would stick fast and drown. He gulped as much air as he could, knowing that he might not have the opportunity to do so for much longer. He fought to swim against the current, hoping to bring himself to a standstill if not to get back to the well-shaft—but he was weaker than he had imagined. The men of Is were famed in Brittany as strong swimmers, but even the strongest of them would have floundered had he been brought as close to dehydration and exhaustion as Edmond Kerval was.

So far as he could judge, the tunnel through which he was being carried was almost level, and there was at least an arm's-length of clearance above the surface, filled with stagnant but breathable air. He was wise enough to know, however, that water would not flow as fast as this along a nearly-level course unless there were a cataract ahead, and he could already hear the cascade. It might, he supposed, be only as high as a man was tall, or it might descend half way to the centre of the world; all he could do was make ready for the drop, and hope to survive it.

The fast-flowing water hurled him over the edge, and for a moment he almost came clear of the stream. Then he hit the pool below the waterfall, and the breath was knocked out of him. The pool was even colder than the flood that had dumped him into it, and he was grateful for the slight additional shock. He was grateful, too, for the fact that the pool was relatively still once he had drifted away from the cascade. He presumed that it must have an outflow somewhere, but it was relatively tranquil in itself.

Kerval was able to swim now, albeit not very strongly, but he dared not make haste. He had to be wary of swimming straight into an unforgiving rock face or catching an arm or leg on a jutting spur. When his hand finally touched something solid, though, it was a ledge. He soon discovered, in fact, that it was one of a whole series of ledges, arranged in a series.

No! he thought, feeling yet another resurgence of optimism. *Not ledges at all, but steps!*

His guess was correct; a flight of stairs had been cut into the rock, leading down into the water from some mysterious vault. Kerval found that he was able to stand up, albeit rather shakily, and climb out on to the flight of steps. Once he was clear of the water, though, he sat down on one of the steps to rest. He squeezed the cloth of his shirt to make it release the water it had trapped, although the pain in his bloodied hands increased markedly as he tightened his grip, informing him that he had lost a good deal of skin.

I must be in some sort of bath-house! Kerval thought, by way of self-encouragement, although the darkness was absolute, and he might have been anywhere at all. By the time he had scrambled up the whole flight of steps he felt steadier on his feet, although the water he had taken in had made him feel slightly sick as well as slaking his thirst. He began to walk away from the head of the staircase, taking one careful step at a time with his hand extended in the darkness before him, wary of meeting a wall.

He found a wall eventually, after taking a dozen steps, but it was not set squarely across his path. It was set aslant, as if the area at the top of the flight of steps were triangular rather than square. *Of course it narrows*, he told himself. *The space by the side of the water must widen out from a corridor of some kind. If I follow the corridor carefully, I'm bound to find more steps....steps that will lead me, eventually, all the way to the surface, for I must be in the cellars of some sort of building...a public building in a city lost for thousands of years in the heart of the desert, where even Tuaregs do not care to go, unless driven by djinn. Oh, Edmond, Edmond Kerval, how could you ever have doubted dear Étienne Marin's word? Destiny has you firmly in its grip, now, and you must be ready to seize its gifts!*

Kerval was shivering now, and his teeth were chattering madly. He would have been very glad indeed to find another flight of steps at the far end of the corridor into which he had evidently come, but it opened out instead into another wide space, of which he could see not a single detail. Rather than marching forwards he followed the wall, running his hand along it even though his pain-racked fingers soon became thickly slimed with something horrid. He paused to wipe them on his trousers, but the slime was difficult to dislodge even on the wet cloth.

When he came to another narrow opening he had no way of knowing whether the tunnel would lead him up or down, but he tried it anyway. There was a wooden door at its further end, which seemed to have been barred or bolted on the other side—at least, he could find no trace of a handle or a lock on his own side, and it would not yield to a tentative push. What gave him hope, though, was the fact that the invisible surface seemed to be covered in slime and fungal nodules. He concluded that it must be rotten, and that if only he could find its weakest point he might be able to make a hole. If he could not dislodge the bar thereafter, he could probably widen the hole bit by bit, until it was large enough to crawl through.

It was hard work, especially for a man in his depleted condition. When the wood finally began to splinter it produced dagger-sharp pieces. They would have been easy enough to avoid had he been able to see them, but under cover of darkness they stabbed his hands and forearms, reopening the cuts that he had sustained while falling down the well and making several new and deeper ones. Even so, such was his desperation and determination that it took him less than an hour to make a way through.

The other side of the door was dry, so Kerval knew that the air beyond it must be contiguous with the desert air through which he had been riding for days. The prospect of dry warmth suddenly seemed very welcoming, so he set off with a will into the darkness, hoping all the while for a glimpse of starlight. The corridor-wall he was now following took him right, then left, and then right again, but it eventually delivered him into yet another open space—and here, at last, he saw chinks of light far above him, let in by narrow horizontal slits that did not seem much like any window he had ever seen before. The still air was much warmer now, and so dry that the water was already evaporating from his clothing.

Kerval might have felt less disappointed by the fact that the floor on which he walked was still lost in darkness had it not been for the fact that his ears had also become active again. He heard a brief flutter of lazy wings, which disturbed him momentarily, because he knew that they probably belonged to roosting vultures.

There were other sounds, though, that were even more disturbing: the sound of serpentine scales slithering on stone, and the click of insectile feet that might belong to scorpions. The latter seemed to be heading towards him, but when he froze and pressed himself against the wall he realized that they were passing by. It was not the scent of his sluggishly-flowing blood that had attracted them but the draught of cooler and moister air that had followed him all the way from the broken door.

When he moved on again, Kerval eventually bumped into a raised stone platform of some kind, whose slightly concave surface was as broad and long as a princely bed, and seemingly quite clean. It was a welcome discovery, for it seemed quite safe from snakes and scorpions alike, which had no way to climb its smooth sides. Desperately tired and weakened by the blood that was still leaking from his hands and arms, Kerval hauled himself up on to the slab and stretched himself out.

Utterly exhausted, but no longer wringing wet or frozen half to death, he fell unconscious almost immediately.

4.

Frustrated and annoyed, Ahmad Meljul got to his feet. He dusted himself down and pulled the broken rope back up. It was only a few inches shorter now than it had been before, but there was no obvious place to secure the free end. The Arab knew that if Kerval were alive and unhurt, the Breton's curses ought to be clearly audible, but no sound emerged from the dark shaft—which suggested that his erstwhile companion must have been knocked unconscious, and quite possibly drowned.

That was a direly uncomfortable thought. The chances of two men outwitting and outfighting half a dozen Tuaregs and as many walking skeletons were poor enough, but the odds against one man doing it were tremendous—and they would become even more astronomical if Meljul could not bring up enough water for himself and the two horses without wasting too much time.

Meljul knew that he had to extend the length of the rope far enough to enable him to tie a bottle to its far end and dangle it in the water. Eventually, he contrived a considerable extension by using his own belt, the sword-belt that Kerval had prudently taken off, and the reins of both the horses. He found that, by leaning over the edge of the hole, with his arm at full stretch, he could get a bottle down to the surface of the water—but filling it up was a different matter. The only bottles he had were made of stiff leather, and they were not heavy enough when empty to sink beneath the surface—and there did not seem to be anyone down there who could push them under for him.

In the end, the best Meljul could contrive was to send down his shirt and bring it back wet. He was glad, though slightly puzzled, to find that the water was not at all brackish or bloodied—but he did not have time to waste in wondering what could possibly have become of Edmond Kerval. He wrung enough water out of the garment to fill his mouth twice over and moisten his head after only one immersion, but satisfying the thirst of the two horses was a task of a very different order. Having no alternative, he set to it with a will, as glad of the darkness of night as he was of the faint light of a crescent moon and the stars, which made it less than absolute.

When he finally felt that he and the two animals were capable of moving on, the Arab carefully replaced the capstone on the well, and then tried to conceal it as best he could. He buckled both belts about his waist, making sure that Kerval's sheathed sword and pouch were quite secure. Then he used the rope and various items of harness to hitch the two horses to the dying camel. When they began to drag it away, with difficulty, he scuffed the sand as best he could to cover the peculiar track its body left behind. He forced the horses to drag its body some distance away, into a narrow gully, before he finished it off, choking it in order to avoid letting the scent of spilled blood to flood into the air. He hesitated over the wisdom of butchering it, but finally concluded that it was worth the risk. He loaded up the best of the meat, and left the rest for the vultures.

Meljul did what he could to obscure the fact that he had lingered so long in the gully, but he knew that his pursuers would need to be unusually stupid not to discover the fact. If the Tuaregs found the well, they had enough men to leave it guarded while they sent search-parties after him. He, alas, could not risk staying nearby—but if there were a well here in addition to as a road, he thought, there must once have been a village, or a town...or even a city like the one of which the crazy Breton had heard rumor. The dunes must have covered the ruins of its buildings hereabouts, but if it had been a place of any considerable size there might be walls still standing only a little further on.

The Arab was glad to have a reason to proceed, and to hope that he might still have a chance of evading his pursuers. Even a city fallen into ruins a thousand years before might offer useful hiding-places, and places where horses with leather socks to protect their hooves might leave no trace of their passage. With luck, it might be a place where traps could be set, and a war of attrition waged with a slender chance of ultimate success, even by one warrior pitted against a dozen, if the one were clever enough and the twelve as stupid as one might reasonably expect of the resurrected dead.

If this was a city once, Meljul thought, *it must have been prosperous in Suleiman's day and long before, when the djinn last had an empire of sorts hereabouts, and were the bane of good men's lives. If those troublesome djinn have indeed returned, this might well be one of the places to which they have returned in force, expecting to find far more than the barest outlines of ruins. I might be walking into a trap—but what choice do I have, when I cannot turn back, and will undoubtedly be caught if I stay here? Men lived alongside the djinn once, albeit not in harmony; how terrible can they really be?*

Meljul found that there were indeed walls only a little further on. The sand had covered most of them, but the stumps of hundreds of fallen columns still projected from the rubble. What must once have been an arterial road was littered now with all manner of stony debris, but it was not too difficult, even in the faintest of moonlight, to pick a course towards the few distant buildings that still seemed more-or-less intact.

There were more signs of life here than there had been among the windswept dunes, but the creepers that overgrew a few of the columns, and the thick-boled trees that grew beside the ancient highway, were understandably parsimonious in the matter of putting forth foliage or fruit.

The stars seemed to shine a little brighter now as the Harmattan's dust settled gradually back to earth in the stillness of the night. The silence was oppressive, though, and the ruined city seemed utterly devoid of life. Any nocturnal hunters that might be prowling among the ruins would obviously take care to be discreet, but Meljul doubted that the vegetation hereabouts was adequate to support a great many herbivores. There might be rats and lizards, which might, in their turn, support a few snakes and jackals, but this region of the empire of death did not seemed to have been stirred by any breath of reanimation just yet—except, of course, for Meljul himself, and his two horses.

He had headed towards the buildings because they offered the best chance of finding a hiding-place where he might safely sleep, but the closer he came to them the less welcoming they seemed. Their long-collapsed, sand-scoured walls seemed uncannily bright and baleful in the near-obscurity, and when the crescent moon set, their dark bulk seemed even more ominous.

The Arab reined in the horses and looked back. For the last thirty paces or so he and the two animals had been walking on smooth bare rock, leaving little or no sign of their passage, and there was more bare rock ahead. If the Tuaregs followed his tracks to this point, they would assume that he had gone straight on towards the buildings in search of shelter. Perhaps, he decided, it was time to make a sly detour.

Meljul set off at a right-angle to his former course, sticking to the smoothest and hardest ground he could find until he had put a good distance between himself and the ancient roadway. Then he cast about until he found a convenient covert between two fallen columns, where even a man with two horses would be invisible to anyone more than twenty paces away in any direction. Satisfied that he could not be found by any but the most monstrous stroke of ill-fortune, Ahmad Meljul then unburdened the two horses and threw himself down on the ground to sleep.

Sleep, however, did not come easily. He did not actually believe what he had told Kerval about the return of the djinn, and he had tried with all his might to keep a tone of levity in his thoughts on the subject, but he was desert-bred, and the folklore of the desert was deeply ingrained in his soul—and he had seen those skull-like faces, which were surely no mere masks. Once again, he found himself wondering whether it might be possible to make pacts with djinn, and whether, if it were, djinn were likely to make significantly worse masters than human beings. The merchants whose wrath he had been forced to flee, having killed one of their number, had not been the first to cause him dire offense, although they had been the first to tip him over the edge of sanity and put a price on his head.

"Perhaps," he murmured, speaking aloud this time in order to have the comfort of hearing his own voice, "the djinn were not such an unmitigated curse upon the land as their victorious human adversaries were delighted to make out once they were safely bound. Perhaps their exile turned once-fertile lands to desert, not because of any curse they laid upon it before being put away, but simply because their labor or wisdom had previously helped the rivers flow that nourished the land. Perhaps the return of the djinn might revitalize the land as well as bringing the dead back from their graves to serve as slaves. Perhaps, if the legendary Land of the Dead is to thrive again, there will be room again for the living within it—and perhaps the djinn might find good use for a clever bowman, especially a fallen aristocrat who has seen as much of the world as I have. Things must have changed in a thousand years, and the returning djinn will need education as to the present state of its affairs."

He paused for further reflection, and then tried once again to go to sleep. He had better luck this time, and might already have been a little delirious when he spoke again, to say: "If any djinni is listening in the darkness, a little lost and a trifle bewildered, hear my words: only save me from the Tuaregs that are hunting me down, and I shall be glad to give you whatever assistance I can to make sense of the new order of things. I have traveled the Mediterranean coastline from end to end in the south, and have seen not a little of the north, which experience has shown me as much of modern civilization as any man might see and understand. If there are contracts to be made with those who have returned, I offer my services gladly."

He certainly went to sleep as soon as he had completed this speech, and was close enough to that state while making it to remember it in the morning as if it had been a dream rather than a reality—but he did not forget it, and he did not repent it either.

5.

Edmond Kerval woke up with a start when a spider ran across his face. He could feel the warmth of a gentle ray of sunlight on his face, but as soon as he sat up, the sensation vanished. His eyes were glued shut and he had to rub them before he could begin to force them open—but the knuckles with which he rubbed them were covered in something glutinous themselves, and when he finally got one eye open he saw that they were caked with a horrid mixture of blood and dried slime. The ends of his fingers were raw, and the joints were painful when he flexed them.

The light that was filtering through a dozen high-set fissures in a huge series of walls—some of which apertures had been deliberately framed as loopholes—was bright enough in itself, but the space in which Kerval found himself was so vast and so cluttered that most of the sunbeams seemed to be soaked up and nullified, so he paid his surroundings scant attention at first. He inspected his hands and forearms instead, and then his clothing.

He was a sorry sight, to be sure. His shirt and trousers hung in tatters, and the bare flesh was scraped and cut wherever it showed through. The panic he felt when he saw that he did not have his sword-belt was only partly assuaged when he remembered that he had taken it off in order to make his brave descent into the well. He remembered that he had taken off his pouch, too, and that all his worldly possessions—such as they were—had been entrusted to the care of an Arab caravan-guard. He sighed, but he was not too dismayed; given that he was still alive, there was a chance that he would see Ahmad Meljul again, and would certainly be welcomed delightedly if he did.

"I'm alive, intact and rested," he said, aloud, in order that he might have the comfort of hearing a human voice—albeit one that was hoarse and feeble.

He forced the other eye open, at last, and then looked around.

Kerval knew immediately that he must be in some sort of temple. Two rows of fluted columns extended before him, to either side of what must once have been an area in which the faithful made their devotions. The floor had been covered in tiles, but the vast majority of them had been displaced—some, apparently, by violence, the rest by the gradual upthrust of sprawling roots.

The open space had been colonized by six gigantic trees of incalculable antiquity, whose crowns were as remarkable for their patchiness as their boles were for their girth. Wherever a beam of light shone through the loopholes or the many cracks in the walls and roof, leaves gathered to receive it, distributing themselves along arcs mirroring the sun's path across the sky—but wherever no direct sunlight ever shone, the tentative branches were bare and shriveled.

Kerval knew that trees needed water as well as light; if it had to be reckoned astonishing that these sprawling excrescences had grown so massive with such a meager supply of light, how much more astonishing was it that their roots must extend deeply into the ground to reach the underground river that had carried him here? He had opened a passageway by breaking a door, but these trees had enjoyed no such luxury: they had obtained their nourishment the hard way, burrowing through stony foundations and the rock beneath.

"It could be worse," he told himself. "There is life here, and I'm sheltered from the heat and hazards of the desert. The walls and roof might be full of cracks, but all the holes are high up, beyond the reach of predatory animals and men. Furthermore, I'm in exactly the kind of place where treasures are often to be fond, if the lore of legend and romance has any foundation at all."

Between the pillars of the colonnade there were squat statues. They were almost totally obscured by the trees that had grown around them, as if hugging them lovingly with their branches, but they were certainly idols of some sort. It was almost impossible, in the circumstances, to make out their shapes, but Kerval got the impression that some resembled squatting toads with horns like cattle, while others were more like biped crocodiles, others more like giant bats, and few like seated apes with more-than-half-human faces, although they too had horns on either side of their foreheads. All of the figures, however—even the toad-like ones—had slight but disturbing implication of humanity about them, as if they were all chimerical hybrids of human and animal elements.

Kerval found himself taking particular note of anything that resembled horns, however faintly, because his cousin Étienne Marin had mentioned horns in connection with gems, and he was, after all, in a place where treasure might be found—if the lore of legend and romance had any trustworthy foundation.

Unfortunately, there was no trace of anything resembling a gem in any of the places where the foreheads of these vaguely-outlined creatures might have been. All that Kerval's inquisitive eyes could discern among the labyrinthine branches was that each of the figures appeared to have a single huge breast, as if they were female on one side of the body and male on the other. It would have been difficult to confirm this hypothesis even if he had been able to see the groins of the statues, and he did not try, because he did not think it at all important. Instead, he scanned the trees scrupulously for any sign of edible fruit. Alas, he found none. Then he peered at the distant walls, his anxious, squinting gaze questing for a doorway or a low window. The temple appeared to be octagonal in shape, although it was difficult to be certain with so much dead vegetation shielding the walls.

Although the trees were obscuring his line of sight, Kerval could just about make out the place where the main doors of the temple must have been. The space within the arched portal appeared to be blocked up, though—not by random vegetation but by virtue of a massed barricade of stone blocks. It was easy to see where the windows had once been, but they seemed to have been blocked off too, at least in their lower ranks. All of the multitudinous shafts of daylight he could see were entering through gaps set at least three times his own height from the floor, most of them just under the eaves or actually in the fabric of the roof. He was not overly worried by this discovery, because the trees were extending their sturdiest branches to all those points of ingress. There were several that would be easily accessible to an agile and determined man, if he were prepared to take a little trouble in climbing up, and there would be time later to consider the problem of getting down on the outside.

"I'll have a way out when I need one," he told himself, his voice becoming a little smoother as he worked saliva into his mouth. "How much better could things be?"

It was only after observing all this that Edmond Kerval looked down at the shallow bowl in which he had curled himself up to spend the night, and guessed that it must have been an altar: a *sacrificial* altar, in which far more blood might once have been spilled than the few clotted droplets he had recently shed....although, as he studied the mess he had made as he turned over in his sleep, those dried-up libations seemed a far from trivial loss. *I must have been exhausted*, he thought, not caring to voice this particular thought aloud, *not to have woken up screaming in pain—but I cannot even remember whether I had nightmares.*

Having realized that the platform was an altar, the Breton turned around to look at the previously-unseen figure that loomed above it. This time, the thrill of panic raised by the sight was not so easily quelled, even though it was intimately alloyed with a thrill of exultation. He saw the treasure immediately—but he also saw the hand that was holding the treasure.

Unlike the smaller figures in the colonnade, the vast idol at which he was staring in dumbstruck amazement was not overgrown, nor had its shape been much eroded by the ages. The representation was of a clothed figure rather than a naked one, and it was more humanlike in other ways. The outline of a single huge breast could be seen on the right side of its body, only partly hidden by an open-necked jacket which might have been intended to resemble a knitted garment, or perhaps chain-mail armor. The left half of the torso was, however, unmistakably masculine in its musculature. Residual flecks of color suggested that the carved clothing might once have been painted, probably in vivid reds and dark blues, while the flesh had been tinted gold.

The idol's face was strangely handsome, in spite of its asymmetry; it was surrounded by a flowing mane of hair that was still stained jet black. The forehead bore yet another pair of long straight horns, spiraled like those sometimes attributed by illuminators to legendary unicorns, but there was no jewel set between them. The treasure that the idol held comprised a dense cluster of gems decorating the head of the scepter—or was it a mace?—that was gripped in its left hand, as if in an ominously threatening gesture caught by the stoppage of time and suspended for centuries.

Most of the gems making up the treasure were colorless, but some were red and some were blue. *Diamonds, rubies, sapphires!* Kerval thought, as he took note that even the shaft of the scepter seemed to be made of green jade. Once again, he began to speak his thoughts aloud, for the sake of reassurance, as he went on: "Just waiting to be collected. The idol may pretend to offer a threat, but it is impotent. It may look as if it is about to strike me dead and pulverize me in its unholy mortar, but that is mere appearance. In fact, it is offering me a reward, with all the generosity of which Fate is capable."

The Breton was avid to possess those gems, but he could see that the scepter would not easily be snapped off, nor the individual gems easily prized loose, even if he were able to find a means of reaching it. Alas, the arm holding the scepter, raised as if in threat, was too high for him to grasp. The other arm—the right, belonging to the female half of the idol, was reaching downwards, and its enormous fingers were within easy reach of his own tiny hand, but the prospect of trying to climb up that arm and across the idol's shoulders, in order to reach the other, was by no means attractive.

While Kerval considered the difficulty of reaching the treasure, he could not help wondering why—if the temple really had been here for thousands of years, and the gemstones really were authentic—the scepter had not been snapped off long ago, or the jewels broken away from it one by one, with the aid of ladders or some other ingenious devices of human engineering.

In the end, he shrugged his shoulders. There were more urgent needs to be supplied before he could even begin to make plans to improvise a sledgehammer or a lever, and a ladder that could take him up to his objective. Most important of all, he needed something to drink.

Kerval knew that abundant water was not far away, but he also knew that he had no alternative but to grope his way towards it in the dark; the daylight entering the building via the flaws in its structure could not possibly reach into the temple's subterranean workings. He could have made up a bundle of dead twigs easily enough, but he had no means of lighting it to make a torch, because his flint-lock and kindling-wool were in his pouch.

He let himself down from the altar, and looked around for the entrance to the corridor that would take him—if he could remember the turns he had made—to the door that he had broken. He saw his footprints easily enough, limned in blood and slime, but one of the shafts of light that illuminated them winked out as he studied their direction, and then another. He looked up at the holes through which the light had come, and saw to his dismay that two of the loopholes were now partly-occluded by cowled and veiled heads. Half-hidden though he was, the two Tuaregs saw him almost immediately, and began calling to their companions in triumphant excitement.

Kerval realized, to his horror, that the same branches that would probably have allowed him to climb up to the gaps, given time and a certain amount of skill, might easily allow the Tuaregs—or, at the very least, their skeletally lean companions—to climb down. Given that he had no weapon, and had been so badly bruised when he fell into the underground river, he could not possibly fight them.

He had no alternative but to flee, and there was no direction in which he might flee but downwards. He had to return to the under-world beneath the temple, not merely to get a drink of water but to search for a hidden means of egress—even if that meant casting himself into the underground river again, and letting it bear him away into the bowels of the Earth. That did not strike him as a pleasant way to die—but the prospect of allowing himself to be cap-tured by the Tuaregs and their uncanny allies seemed even worse.

"Damn you, Étienne Marin!" he exclaimed, quietly, but with feeling, as he moved back into the darkness. "Damn you for repeat-ing some stupid traveler's tale as if it were your own adventure, to make yourself look better in the eyes of innocent children—and damn you, too, for finding a second-hand tale that had a grain of truth in it, and was all-too-well-designed to lead those innocents to their doom!"

6.

When Ahmad Meljul found the tracks along the roadway, soon after first light, his first impulse was to curse—and he did so volubly, elaborate cursing being a particular art and delight of his people. The tracks told him, unambiguously, that the Tuaregs and the ambulant skeletons had traveled all through the night, so determined were they that their prey should not escape. What was worse, he could only find traces of the passage of six camels; the other six must have been left behind—almost certainly at the well.

The discovery that the enemy's forces had been divided into two equal parties might have given him some encouragement had Kerval still been with him, but while he was alone, the odds against him would need further reduction before he had any chance of winning a fight at close quarters. He cursed that realization too. Once his bad temper had been purged by the cursing, though, he dutifully counted his blessings. His pursuers had not realized that he had moved away from the road in order to rest—or, if they had realized it, had not been able to locate the traces of his detour in the darkness. That was fortunate. And the enemy was divided now, which would make it easier to wage a war of attrition against them.

"So be it," he murmured. "If one man must contend against twelve, six of which are probably something worse than men, then the one must slay the six that can still be killed, and deal with the rest as circumstance demands. If Allah wills that he shall be victorious, the one man will prevail."

He hid the horses as best he could; the necessity of stealth required that he go forward on foot. He was tempted to go towards the well, where the immediate reward of an initial victory would doubtless be greater, but he knew that the Tuaregs would expect him to do exactly that. The guardians of the well would affect insouciance, but they would be eternally on their guard, covertly watchful and ready to react to the slightest sign of an enemy's proximity. By the same token, the party that had gone on ahead would still be hopeful that he might be ahead of them, ripe for ambush himself.

Meljul turned towards the distant buildings whose pink roofs were already catching the light from the rising sun. The sun was yellow and the sky clear blue; the Harmattan had died down during the tranquil night—but there was already a hint of movement in the air, which might soon become a breeze, and then the kind of wind that sent sandstorms forth to scour the desert clean of the echoes of human workmanship. Such scouring was the work of centuries, but it was inexorable—or had been, for the last thousand years. If the djinn really were returning, things might be different from now on.

The Arab cursed again when he first caught sight of the Tuaregs—although he might have thanked Allah instead, had he been so minded, for he had certainly caught sight of them before they had caught sight of him, and they were so deeply engrossed in a new discovery that they were not looking behind them at all.

They had found a building whose shell was still intact, even to the extent that its roof had not yet collapsed. It was the only one for miles around, almost certainly the only one in the entire dead city. It must have been a palace or a temple—probably the latter. In the days when men had lived here, probably in the very borders of the ancient Land of the Dead, they had taken their gods—or, in modern reckoning, the djinn they chose to worship in preference to the One True God—far more seriously than their kings, and rightly so. For a thousand years now, and perhaps far more, if the lapse of time to which the legend referred was merely a convenient way of indicating a lapse too vast to be calculable or imaginable, the power of human kings and emperors had been relatively unchecked, but things had been different in the antiquity of myth.

Ahmad Meljul crouched down in a covert, after making sure that his head would not be outlined against the sky while he made his observations. Then, with a judicious sequence of swift glimpses, he took careful stock of the situation. The immense building was an octagonal structure, whose design was conspicuously different from the architectural styles of Araby. A great deal of sand had piled up against one of its two west-facing walls—so much sand, in fact, that the accumulation could not possibly have been natural. There had to be a substantial amount of rubble beneath the sand, deliberately accumulated and shored up in order to form the foundation of an artificial slope. The rubble had not come from the building itself, since its walls and roof were almost completely intact, so it must have been transported from a distance, at the expense of a great deal of labor—certainly not the work of the Tuaregs who were presently testing the slope.

Someone, at some time, was very enthusiastic to make a way into that place, Meljul told himself, considering the matter with due deductive care. *It must have taken far more effort to pile up that debris than to batter down the door, if the door were unimpeded, so the door must have been braced and barricaded within, perhaps at the same time, perhaps at a much earlier date. Given that the slope presently gives access to two of the high windows, it must be assumed that whoever built it did, in fact, gain access to the building, letting themselves down inside with the aid of ropes. Then they went away again, presumably having found what they were looking for and taking possession of it. Unless....*

He stopped there. The past did not matter. What mattered was the present, and the fact that the Tuaregs and their allies had already divided their forces again. Two of the Tuaregs had climbed to the top of the rather treacherous slope, and they were presently craning their necks towards the gaps in the building's fabric, eager to peep through. One other Tuareg and three other humanoid figures were waiting at the bottom of the slope with six camels. The three who were not human—or not entirely human, at any rate—gave the impression of being impatient. They did not seem at all eager to climb up the slope themselves, but the two men at the top were already calling excitedly down to the third Tuareg, demanding tools with which to make the cracks around the loopholes even wider.

What have they seen within? Meljul wondered. *What could distract them from a vengeful hunt? The slender ones with the fleshless faces seem enthusiastic to go on, but the Tuaregs have discovered a different agenda. They too have heard the kind of tale that drew the Breton here; they are human, and they have human dreams of fortune and enrichment, of fabulous good fortune gifted by Allah to those he favors. Whatever they have seen, it has awakened dreams of avarice!*

Meljul knew that what the Breton's cousin was supposed to have said about idols with gems for eyes was the standard stuff of all traveler's tales, including those that circulated in the souks of Araby. He also knew, however, that there really *were* cities buried in the desert sands, relics of a time when the desert had not been as arid as it was now. The world was very ancient; it had been inhabited long before the rise of the present human civilization, and long before the rise of *any* civilization. The abandoned cities of Araby itself had been looted long ago, but the borderlands of the so-called Land of the Dead had long been let alone, even by the Tuaregs—whose rise to civilization, if it could not be reckoned definitely stillborn, evidently had yet to begin. These particular Tuaregs would know the market value of gems well enough, but their ancestors had probably learned that value from caravan-masters within the last dozen generations ago. It was certainly conceivable that a temple like this one might have been here for thousands of years, its existence unknown to anyone with sufficient intelligence to be an efficient looter—but *this* temple *had* been discovered, by individuals with sufficient organization and determination to fabricate a way in. Looters had been here before—so why were the Tuaregs getting excited?

This is foolish! Meljul chided himself. *The point is that at least two, and perhaps more, of the six adversaries before me are about to go into the building. When they do, I shall be one against four, three, or perhaps even two. I should be able to strike at least two with my arrows before they can make any profitable response—but if the skull-faces really are reanimated dead men, will arrows stop them?*

He would have been glad of the opportunity to act swiftly, but the two Tuaregs at the top of the slope were coming down now, eager to fetch equipment that would help them make the internal descent. When they arrived at the bottom, they immediately became embroiled in an argument with their strange companions, who obviously did not have authority enough over their human allies to demand obedience. While the squabble went on, Meljul found himself drawn irresistibly back to the question of treasure, and all the old stories that were designed specifically to intrigue and capture the human imagination.

There is only one reason, according to the lore of legend, why great treasures remain long unlooted, he reminded himself, *and that is that they are exceedingly well-guarded.*

Even that conjecture endorsed one more item to the account that Étienne Marin had given his cousin, and the countless similar tales that were retailed about camp-fires when caravans paused at oases. According to Kerval, his cousin had sworn that, although he had clearly seen the gems of which he spoke, he had been quite unable to reach them, because they were guarded by monsters—monsters, in this particular instance, like crocodiles with eyes of fire that walked erect on their hind legs. The last detail, at least, Meljul thought, had surely to be false—not so much because he could not believe that there was any such thing as a crocodile that walked erect, but because there was every reason to believe that there was not enough food and water hereabouts to support such creatures, even if they did exist.

Or was there? The water in the well, he remembered, had seemed to be in motion when he had lowered his shirt into it. Was it possible that it was an underground river, flowing all the way from the distant mountains? Was it possible that the river harbored life—fish of some sort?

Meljul cursed himself as a fool. "No light, no life," he murmured. "No fish, no crocodiles." He forced himself to concentrate on his immediate enemies.

The Tuaregs seemed to have won the argument. All three of them were making their way up the slope again, armed with various items of equipment. They obviously intended to make a concerted effort to widen the cracked loopholes through which they had peered before, in order that one or more of them could pass through. Meljul was glad to observe that the skull-faces now seemed very uncertain as to what to do. One of them was already climbing up, very tentatively, in pursuit of the Tuaregs, while the others seemed now to be quarreling with one another, or at least engaging in animated discussion. If all four of the climbers contrived to get inside, only two would remain without....

The Arab waited, patiently, shadowed from the sun's glare. He was thirsty, but not yet so desperate for water that his senses were disturbed. His dry lips formed a rictus of satisfaction when he saw one of the two skull-faces turn away from the dispute, mount one of the camels and ride off in the direction of the well. He knew that re-inforcements could not possibly arrive for some time, even if they came in a hurry; the cracks around the loopholes were almost wide enough now to allow the Tuaregs to squeeze through. *Be my guest!* he said, silently. *May you step straight into a nest of horned vipers, or spitting cobras.*

The first of the Tuaregs disappeared, then the second. The clambering skull-face had reached the top of the slope. The time had come to act. Meljul moved swiftly to the position he had selected in advance. He wasted no time once he was there, immediately flexing his bow to secure the string, then plucking an arrow from his quiver.

The third Tuareg had gone into the temple, and the skull-face was peering after them, hesitantly. Meljul took careful aim at the lone skull-face at the foot of the slope, and let fly. The shot was per-fect: the arrow ploughed into the target's back, tearing through the skull-face's loosely-fitting robe. If the creature had kidneys, the barbed arrow-head must be ripping through the one on the right, slashing its blood-vessels and pulverizing its tissues.

The slender body arched, exactly like that of a man struck in the back by a well-directed arrow, and then fell backwards, seemingly inert—or at the very least, hurt and disabled. Although the injured creature had not screamed, there must have been sound enough to warn its companion, which immediately turned away from the fis-sure in the building's wall—but the Tuaregs who had weakened the wall in order to widen the gap had obtained greater success than they had known or hoped. A considerable block of stone suddenly fell inwards, its supporting structure having been fatally weakened, and it took the rubble at the very top of the slope with it. The skull-face perched there was awkwardly unbalanced; it teetered and waved its emaciated arms, but it could not stay upright—and when it fell, it tumbled down inside the building rather than outside.

This time, Meljul was not slow to thank Allah for his bounty as he ran down the slope towards the five untended camels.

He knew full well, as he ran, that the sensible course of action was to mount one of the beasts, seize the reins of the others, and gal-

lop southwards with all the booty that was still attached to their sad-
dle-bags, riding full-tilt into the unknown for at least an hour before
slowing down and making concerted attempts to cover or confuse
his tracks. He knew that—but he was an aristocrat among Arabs, in
spite of the low estate to which he had fallen, and he had never sat
on a camel in his life, in spite of having served long years as a caravan-master's mercenary—and there was a voice in his head that was
urging him to take a look into the temple himself, partly because he
wanted to see whatever the Tuaregs had seen, and partly because the
Tuaregs might be trapped inside, easy targets for a bowman of his
prowess.

If he could kill three more of his potential pursuers before taking flight, his ultimate task might become a great deal easier.

For these reasons, therefore, he only paused by the camels long
enough to take a long look at the creature he had felled—and as he
went to do that, he seized a water-skin, in order to take a long, luxu-
rious drink.

The skull-face turned out to be somewhat more than a death's-
head. The dark eye-sockets were not empty, but harbored eyes of a
sort: vitreous black orbs. The lipless mouth, gaping open in response
to the shock of the arrow's impact, had a black tongue within. When
Meljul parted the creature's robes, he found that the rib-cage was
covered with a thin layer of translucent skin, and that it visibly contained organs similar to a human's: a heart, a stomach, lungs....

The creature had kidneys, too, but they had not shed any blood
where the arrow had gone in. The creature did, however, seem to be
well and truly dead.

"If you are indeed a reanimated corpse, and not some strangely-
transfigured living man," Meljul said, staring into the sinister black
eyes, "at least your reanimation does not seem to have gifted you
with immortality. May Allah make certain that you stay dead this
time, though." He retrieved his arrow and returned it to his quiver.
Then he attached the water-bottle, still half-full, to his belt. His
waist was now over-crowded, because he was still wearing Kerval's
sword and belt as well as his own, but he thought it worth the incon-
venience.

When he looked up the slope at close range, Meljul saw that his earlier surmise had been correct. The hill had, indeed, been contrived by many sets of human hands. The ancient debris had been rather hastily arranged, so that the steep ramp must have been treacherous even when it was new, but it had proved sturdy enough to remain in place and to trap a good deal of windblown sand. It was highly unlikely that Étienne Marin had played any part in that labor, but *some* company of treasure-hunters had done it, and at least one among them must have lived to tell the tale.

Meljul regretted leaving the rope that he had let down into the well with the two horses, because it seemed now that it might be a useful thing to have once he had reached the top of the slope. He wondered, very briefly, whether he ought to return to the horses anyway, and redirect his violent attentions towards the guardians of the well. If more than half of them decided to set off with the skull-face who had gone to summon help, there might only be two or three left behind—and if he could kill them, he would be able to flee northwards rather than southwards, towards the distant reaches of civilization.

On the other hand, he thought, *the only welcome I'll receive in civilization is that of the law's cruelty, and the wrath of my erstwhile masters. The one sure answer to that kind of hostility is money....*

He was, in any case, still determined at least take a look into the interior of the temple; so, having made sure that his bow was secure, Meljul began to climb. He went warily, keeping the gap in view at all times, lest one of the Tuaregs should have been alerted by the sound of the skull-face's fall to the fact that all was not well outside.

The slope was harder to negotiate than it had seemed to his inexpert eye, but Meljul reached the top soon enough. Alas, when he looked into the gloomy interior he did not see a vast empty space and the broken body of a skull-face: he saw a dense tangle of vegetation, replete with footholds and handholds. There was a mess of broken branches marking the skull-face's fall, but there seemed to be every chance that the skull-face had managed to cling on, and then to follow its companions in a measured descent. None of them was visible now, although the interior of the temple was so dark that they might easily be lurking in the shadows, looking up at him.

That thought made the Arab snatch his head back and move back from what was now a very substantial gap, bracing himself gingerly against the wall of the building, wary of the possibility of a further collapse. He paused for a moment, taking advantage of his lofty viewpoint to look out over the sand-drowned ruins. From up here it was much easier to make out the contours of the dead city. He could see other shapes sketched out in the sand, though none were octagonal, and his gaze could trace the remnants of vast colonnades. He saw now that the other structures that protruded most stubbornly from the dunes were mostly pyramids and the stubs of broken statues.

Beyond the city there was a further expanse of shallow dunes: a barren plain that stretched as far as the eye could see. That plain undoubtedly extended far into the fabled Land of the Dead, but there was no sign visible from this vantage-point of any renewal of life there—or whatever kinds of undeath might be substituted for life by the crafts of the liberated djinn. There were more urgent matters demanding Meljul's attention, though, and he turned again to peer discreetly around the edge of the gap into the temple's interior.

A huge tree had directed the strongest and leafiest part of its crown towards the crack, and some of those branches had undoubtedly provided a safety-net of sorts for the falling skull-face. The thin-limbed creature was certainly too light to crash through the net, he decided; its fall had obviously been interrupted, and the branches had then offered abundant handholds, even to a creature as uneasy in its balance as the skull-face seemed to be. Instead of falling to its second death, the skull-face must still be in a fit state to make profitable use of its substitute life. But where was it now? And where were the three Tuaregs?

It was not easy to see through the clustered foliage, even when his eyes had become more comfortably adjusted to the obscurity, but there seemed to be statues set between the columns supporting the roof, and one unusually large erection set against the far wall of the building. It was impossible for Meljul to discern the shape of that principal idol from his current vantage-point, but its left arm was clearly visible, including the upraised hand, and in that hand was a scepter, whose head was sparkling with variously-colored fire—not,

Ahmad Meljul thought, because it was reflecting a fugitive shaft of sunlight, but because it was *glowing*. It was almost as if that upraised hand were advertising the presence of the scepter to anyone or anything who might chance to peep through this particular aperture—but also issuing a brutal threat to anyone who might have the temerity to come in and take it.

7.

Edmond Kerval moved into the dark corridor anxiously, knowing that he was likely to be at a double disadvantage when his enemies came after him. The Tuaregs and their slender allies—who would doubtless outnumber him even if they left some of their number to stand guard without—were well-armed, while he had nothing now with which to defend himself but his sore hands. In addition, the Tuaregs would undoubtedly have the means to strike a light, and no shortage of materials with which to improvise torches. When they followed him into the darkness, as they undoubtedly would, they would be able to see where they were going. He could not.

He went into the darkness anyway, knowing that he had to find his way back to the pool from which he had emerged on the previous evening, so that at least he might have a drink of water before he made further plans.

It's not so bad, he told himself. *If they can light their way, then I shall be able to see them coming before they see me. If these corridors are labyrinthine, they may split up in order to search for me—and who knows what might have been stored down here, behind that door that I was the first in a thousand years to break? There might be weapons that I can appropriate. I might even be able to set traps.*

He did not remind himself that there might already be traps set to catch intruders like himself, and worse things. He could not help remembering, though, that Étienne Marin had taken the trouble to mention monstrous crocodiles. Was it possible that the underground river that had brought him here harbored such predators, and that they used the temple as a roost?

No, he told himself, *it is not. Have I not already navigated the underground river, and the pool beneath the temple, in perfect safe-*

ty, despite being quite unable to see? If there were hungry beasts in the vicinity, they would surely have made a meal of me while I was wet and helpless.

He groped his way along the wall, wincing at the effects which the friction had on his cuts and grazes. He turned without hesitation whenever he came to a junction, but he knew by the time that he had made five such turns that he could not possibly be retracing his steps of the previous night. If he had been returning the way he had come, he would have come to the broken door by now.

He paused and took stock of his position, listening hard and trying to detect a draught in the air. He could hear sounds, which were presumably coming from the temple, where the Tuaregs must now have made their descent along the tree-branches—but he could also feel a cool current in the air, which must surely be coming from the vaults below. He set himself to face the airflow, and moved off again.

Every time he reached a junction thereafter, he paused to consider the possibilities carefully. Within a quarter of an hour he had found the door again, and had not yet seen a flicker of light behind him. After that, it was easy enough to find the first flight of steps, and then the second. He picked his way down very carefully, until his feet finally encountered the water, and then he knelt down to drink. For the moment, nothing else mattered as much as that.

By the time he had drunk his fill, Kerval could hear louder sounds, which echoed strangely in the subterranean corridors. It appeared that his pursuers were arguing—or, at least, exclaiming over something. He heard the clink of metal on stone, and knew that the blades in question were being plied in earnest rather than merely chancing to come into contact with walls or a floor. Perhaps, he thought, they were being deployed against scorpions and snakes that he had been unable to see, and which had let him pass unhindered because he carried no disturbing light.

His blinking eyes made every effort to stay alert, desperate to catch first faint hint of torchlight in the distance—but that was not the kind of light they eventually saw.

What Edmond Kerval actually caught sight of was a red spot, bright and by no means diffuse: a spot like a cyclopean eye burning with its own inner light. He thought, at first, that it was an illusion produced by the effort that his eyes were making, and the pressure they were exerting on his imagination, but that idea could not sustain its plausibility for long. After blinking a few times, he concluded that the glimmer was definitely real, and that—however absurd it might seem—it was some kind of eye. He had no doubt that it was looking at him, perhaps studying him intently, and perhaps taunting him…or both.

He might have cried out a challenge, but for the certainty of attracting the attention of his pursuers. As things were, he had no alternative but to hold himself very still and silent, meeting the cyclopean stare as courageously as he could, and wondering in the meantime whether he ought to throw himself into the water as soon as he felt a touch of any kind, and start swimming.

What would I give to have my saber in my hand now? he thought. *All the gems in that scepter, I suppose.*

"The price is higher than that," a voice whispered in his ear, making him start violently, "but the potential reward is greater."

Kerval could not help raising his arm and passing at back and forth in an arc. It met nothing but empty air, although the whisperer—had he or it been material—surely could not have been more than a hand's-breadth away from his eardrum. Fortunately, he had the presence of mind not to make any actual sound as his mind framed the natural question: *Can you hear my thoughts?*

"The first gift is sight," the voice went on, as if it were proffering an oblique answer. "The second gift…well, you shall see what the second gift is when you have accepted the first. But the fee you have so far paid to remain in the game is but a tiny drop of water in a large and thirsty throat. You must offer the rest freely, if you wish to play—but you probably have no more than a minute or two to decide before your pursuers appear, and you will not easily pass through the ranks of my faithful servants for a second time."

Fee? Kerval thought. *What fee? And whose ranks have I passed through without knowing it?* The first question, at least, was rhetorical, partly because he already had an inkling as to what the voice must mean by *fee*, and partly because he knew full well that he had little or no time to haggle, even if there were any scope at all for a better bargain to be struck. There was, however, one further question that he was desperate to ask.

Are you one of those demonic djinn which the Solomon of the Old Testament bound in helplessness, now set free again to harass mankind? he asked.

The voice laughed, very softly. "You should not pay so much heed to silly tales," it said. "They will always mislead you, even when they contain grains of truth. The gift of information, too, I shall add to my offer, for no extra charge—but not quite yet. For now, what you need is sight, however terrifying it might prove to be. Without that, you will likely be dead in a matter of minutes. I can gift you an afterlife, of sorts, but I can assure you that you will find it preferable to stay alive a little longer—and you ought to be very grateful that I prefer that outcome too, at least for the present. Time is pressing: decide!"

Kerval knew that there was really no choice at all, and that he was already in "the game", as the merest of pawns, whether he liked it or not. He made his decision. He did not have to frame his consent in words, even of the inaudible kind. Before he was even entirely sure that he had framed the intention, the red glow moved, dividing into two as it rushed upon his eyes, entering into both his wide-dilated and staring pupils simultaneously.

He felt the djinn's sight fuse with his own, gifting him with the sight that the djinn had possessed all along—and he also felt the djinn's intelligence fusing with his own, somehow taking up residence behind his eyes, in what had previously been the sacrosanct privacy of his skull. He did not suppose for an instant, though, that the djinn was imprisoned there, bound by any kind of seal.

At first, he found the djinn's gifted sight dazzling and confusing, but he adapted to its use soon enough. The entire cavern then seemed lit by an eerie red light, so unlike any ordinary illumination that Kerval did not doubt for an instant that no other human being would be able to make use of it. If the Tuaregs' torches went out, they would be blind and he would not; even without his saber, he might be able to do far better than evade them—but what he saw by the power of his new vision, once he was able to discern actually objects, chilled him to the bone far more effectively than the mere sight of an armed Tuareg or another abrupt immersion in the underground river could ever have done.

His eyes were level with the top step of the flight, and hence with the floor-space beyond, which was some twenty paces wide at the stair-head. He had walked across that space twice, keeping near to the wall on each occasion, but it seemed impossible that he could have done so without guidance, for the space was littered with what appeared at first to be crocodiles—eighteen of them, every one of them half as long again as a man was tall. They were all lying down on their bellies, but they were not asleep; their eyes were not merely open but attentive—and they were all looking in his direction. Their snouts and tails were exactly similar to the crocodiles he had seen on the banks of the Nile, but their legs were not—the back ones, in particular, were longer and sturdier.

They could have seized me at any time, he thought. *They let me pass last night, and they let me pass again this morning. They are not slaves of instinct but obedient servants of a master...the entity that is now* my *master.*

The creatures had not stirred as yet, but while he stared down at them and they stared back, their heads began to move from side to side, as if in a gesture of weary disapproval, underlain by sympathy. Somehow, he could not bear to think that they might feel sorry for him, now that his fate was linked to theirs.

The head-shaking did not stop, but it was seamlessly converted into a different kind of movement. The recumbent crocodiles turned their heads, and then began to turn their bodies, to face the opening of the corridor: the opening where a different kind of light was now beginning to show. The new light seemed sulfurously yellow to Kerval's unnatural sight. He saw the flame of the torch before he saw its reflection in the eyes of the first Tuareg.

Kerval knew that the Tuareg could not see him, but he also knew that his invisibility was irrelevant, for the moment—because what the Tuareg *could* see, by the light of his improvised torch, was the crocodiles.

Meljul had assured Kerval more than once that the Tuareg were essentially cowardly—cunning in their cowardice, but cowards nevertheless. Perhaps this one was an exception, or perhaps his cunning was sufficient to outweigh his cowardice, at least for a few vital seconds. The Tuareg howled in anguish, as any human less dumbfounded than Kerval would have done, and certainly did not linger long in the deadly cavern, but he had the presence of mind to lower the torch before he fled, and place it very carefully across the entrance, so that the flames swiftly spread along the whole length of the bundle, thus forming a barrier of fire that no ordinary crocodile would ever have dared to approach, let alone to cross. The trick should have secured the Tuareg's safe retreat—but these were no ordinary crocodiles.

Seemingly irritated by the presence of the flame, the lean monsters reared up, standing on their hind legs, as Kerval had half-anticipated when he saw the sturdiness of those limbs. Their heads were still moving, but they were now swaying back and forth rather than swaying, and their jaws gaped to expose their teeth. What those teeth lacked in mass they made up in profusion—and it seemed to Kerval that there was a definite malice in the reptiles' eyes.

None of the crocodiles turned towards Kerval; instead, they moved as one toward the corridor through which the Tuaregs were fleeing. Their leader stamped on the burning bundle of twigs, extinguishing the flames with the hard pads of its hind feet. All eighteen monsters moved after the invaders who had dared to bring the light of the upper world into their secret realm. They moved unhurriedly, but with every appearance of steadfast purpose.

Kerval knew that he ought to feel thoroughly relieved, and even thankful—but he could not muster the emotional energy.

"What now?" he said, speaking aloud, although he knew that there was no need, simply because he could.

He was not surprised when his own voice answered him, animated by his own breath and his own vocal cords.

"We have a little time in hand," said the djinn who had taken up temporary residence within his brain. "Strange—I had not expected to feel so comfortable here. If all men are now like you, there has been *progress* while I have been asleep. I am delighted to know that—I love progress. It will make the game so much more interesting."

"Asleep?" Kerval queried, determined now to use his voice as and when he could, lest he find himself imprisoned in thought while his new master made free with the privileges of his flesh. "Did Solomon only put you to sleep, then?"

"Suleiman the Great was a mere opportunist," the djinn told him, "who claimed sole credit for what he had not done alone, in order to obtain undeserved prestige and authority over his fellows. He made a bargain such as you have just made, but he made it with Azazel, the Prince of Lies. Azazel was always a cheat, with no real sense of the aesthetics of the game. I suppose we must give him due credit for the sheer scale of his trickery, but I doubt that he obtained as much pleasure from his victory as he anticipated, and I imagine that he must be terrified now of the price he will have to pay for his temerity."

"Azazel is a demon," Kerval deduced. "A demon who stole a march on all his fellows, in an attempt to secure the world of men for his own personal playground."

"The matter is not quite as simple as that," his new demonic master assured him, "but in broad terms, yes. Azazel contrived to send all but a few of us to sleep, by a means that I—and doubtless many others—am direly anxious to discover. He did us no injury, and I cannot deny that there is a certain precious interest in waking up refreshed to a changed world, but the insult cannot go unpunished. You understand that, do you not?"

One thing that Kerval did understand—an idea that he attempted to seize as a drowning man might clutch at a straw—was that by far the greater number of the world's demons had once been rendered inactive, by a means they did not yet understand, and that human life had proceeded, relatively unhindered by their presence, for a thousand years or more. While the means remained unknown to them, he thought, it was not impossible that they might be rendered inactive again, for a similar period.

"Quite so," said his own voice. "And that, my fine new friend, is what has saved your life and your freedom of consciousness, at least for a little while. One thing we do know is that Azazel used human instruments, more cleverly that they had ever been used before—and so must we. That is why I am showering you with valuable gifts, at an exceedingly tiny cost to you."

Kerval felt his heart sink, then, because he knew exactly what price demons were generally supposed to demand in exchange for their gifts, and was beginning to figure out exactly how that price might be paid.

Again, it was his own voice that replied to his anxiety. "Look on the brighter side," his possessor advised him. "Your soul is mine, now—but imagine what your newly-armored flesh and free intelligence might now experience, while you take your place in a magnificent army of the living and the dead, and set forth to do glorious battle. What could any merely human life ever have offered you to compare with that? Be sure, too, that I shall not diminish your own consciousness in the least, until it has taught me everything it can about the way of the new world. Rejoice, and make ready; we have work to do, and a very long way to go."

"May I know your name?" Kerval asked—not so much because he wanted to know, but because he wanted to speak, in order to reassure himself that he was still capable of using his own voice.

"Call me Semiaza," the demon said, "and don't despair. It is not impossible, in the fullness of time, that you will clear your debt to me, and regain the whole of your freedom—for what that might be worth, in a narrow world like yours."

8.

Once Ahmad Meljul's eyes had fully adapted to the dim light inside the temple he was finally able to make out the skulking form of the skull-face, which was still insinuating itself through a tangle of branches towards the idol behind the altar. It was almost as if the creature were being drawn towards the glowing scepter, although Meljul could not believe that it had the same avaricious instincts as its Tuareg allies. The Tuaregs were, however, nowhere to be seen. They had had plenty of time to study the scepter and to set about making some kind of frame that would allow them to climb up to it, in order to begin the work of detaching its glittering head—so the fact that they were not doing so was decidedly odd. Where were they, and what could possibly have distracted them from the lure of the treasure?

Meljul touched his bow thoughtfully, but he did not have a clear shot at the skull-face from where he was, because of the intervening tree-branches. He suspected that he might have to make his own descent to the temple floor in order to find a place from which to take reliable aim, and he did not want to do that. He was about to turn around and go back down the slope, in order to make his escape, when the skull-face finally reached the altar and begin to climb up, looking towards the scepter as it did so. Curiosity got the better of the Arab again, and he hesitated.

Although its slender frame was at least three inches taller than Meljul's, and it had considerably longer arms, the scepter was still frustratingly out of reach when the skull-face stood on tiptoe on the altar. The creature looked around, as if it too were wondering where its companions had gone, and made as if to jump down again—but then it changed its mind. It unsheathed its sword—which was not a scimitar like the blades the Tuaregs carried, but something more akin to an épée—and reached upwards, easily able with its aid to make contact with the scepter. Meljul judged that there was nothing to be achieved by striking at a solid object with a sword as thin as that one—such recklessness could only ruin the blade—but the skull-face had no intention of using brute force; it was content to tap and tease the scepter with the blade, as if it were trying to identify the material of which it was made.

If the creature can find a way to dislodge the scepter's head, Meljul thought, *that might work to my advantage*—but he immediately tried to put the thought out of his mind. His only priority, for the moment, was to make his escape. Perhaps he could return to the city at a later and safer date. *But the scepter will be gone by then,* he could not help adding. *If I leave the Tuaregs and the skull-faces to it, they'll surely figure out a way to break it off in the end, and it will make their fortune….*

That was a deeply frustrating prospect, not merely because of what he would lose, but because of what his despicable enemies would gain. Meljul knew, however, that he really ought not to linger long before taking to his heels, else the skull-face that had returned to the well would return with reinforcements, and he would be lost. He looked around, but he could see no sign of movement in the ruins. Still he hesitated, rocking back on his heels as he watched the skull-face tapping the scepter with its slender blade. The creature seemed to be puzzled, as if the scepter were a particularly vexing enigma.

There must be a booby-trap of some sort, Meljul thought, else the gems would have been stolen long ago. If the skull-face were to fall into it, so that I might be forewarned....

Again he tried to thrust the thought aside, and again met with resistance.

"Perhaps that's the trap," he muttered, aloud. "Perhaps I'm in it too, or at least caught on its threshold, unable to leave, by virtue of some magic. Perhaps the Tuaregs have already been swallowed up."

Nothing happened to the skull-face, though. The creature sheathed its blade again, having obtained no apparent enlightenment from its investigation.

Meljul glanced behind him again, checking the northern horizon for movement. This time he saw something, at the limit of vision: a slight disturbance, but a highly significant one. The Tuareg and their allies had to be traveling quickly enough to stir up a haze of dust even from the stony road. Reinforcements were, indeed, on their way. They were still at least a mile away—which should have been plenty of time for him to run back down the slope, leap astride one of the camels and make his escape—but no sooner had Meljul taken that decision and looked downwards than he realized that his patience had betrayed him.

The skull-face that had seemed conclusively dead when he had inspected its body was now on its feet again. Worse than that, it had taken a bow and a sheaf of arrows from one of the packs that were still on the patient camels' backs. It had already strung the bow, and was fitting an arrow to the string.

"So the dead can return twice—or perhaps a hundred times over!" Meljul muttered, before adding a string of curses, mostly aimed at himself for missing the opportunity that Allah had generously given him.

He considered stringing his own bow, or racing down the slope at full tilt to attack the skull-face, whose movements seemed considerably impaired by the arrow in its back, but he could not possibly shoot first, and any downhill rush would reduce the range at which his opponent's shot would be fired.

Before completing his final curse, Meljul took the prudent course, moving into the gap in the temple wall and jumping into the crown of the nearest tree. He was not so wrapped up in his recriminations that he compounded his error by neglecting further precautions. As he moved from the gap in the eaves into the foliage of the tree he was careful not to disturb any more masonry—wisely so, for he had taken note of the fact that the edges of the hole were very ragged, and that new cracks were already spreading from it as the weight of the temple's roof bore down on the wall. That roof had resisted collapse for an amazingly long time, in spite of the external erosion caused by windblown sand and the internal corrosions of the patient trees, but now that the solidity of the juncture had been rudely breached, it suddenly seemed distinctly precarious, even to the casual judgment of an inexpert eye.

The skull-face on the altar was not yet aware of Meljul's presence, but the possibility of getting to a position from which he could easily put an arrow into the creature's slender back seemed slim even before three Tuaregs suddenly emerged from a dark doorway to the right of the altar, apparently in a state of terrified panic.

Meljul moved swiftly then, knowing that he had to hide himself from the gap behind him and from the floor below, before the wounded skull-face could reach the top of the slope and the Tuaregs recovered sufficient presence of mind to notice his presence. He had to find a position somewhere in the crowded temple from which he could put as many of his enemies down as possible before the second party of camel-riders arrived and the two companies could combine their forces. Given that the skull-faces could only be removed from the battle on a temporary basis, the chances of his survival seemed poorer now than they had ever been before.

Those chances did not seem to have improved much when the situation suddenly became more complicated still. The Tuaregs were followed from the dark doorway by a spectacularly horrid monster:

a crocodile marching on its hind legs, with its forelimbs extended in a menacing gesture. The monster was, however, unarmed, and it was immediately greeted by an arrow and a javelin, both of which weapons sank into its lightly-armored breast.

Meljul cursed—and could not bring himself to take any pleasure in the circumstances when, after a momentary pause, the crocodile continued to waddle forwards regardless of its wounds. When the Arab saw that the monster was not alone, it occurred to him that he might yet be confronted by enemies even worse than the Tuaregs and the skull-faces. He almost jumped back towards the gap—but he stopped when he saw the awful head of the skull-face appear in the breach. He shrank back into hiding instead,

Down below, the second crocodile was followed by a third, and the third by a fourth. No more missiles were hurled at them; the Tuaregs were already searching for footholds in the trees, intending to retreat at least until they were out of easy reach. Meljul wondered, as the tribesmen were also undoubtedly wondering, whether the crocodiles were capable of climbing as well as walking upright. Meanwhile, the skull-face that had jumped down from the altar jumped back up again, and drew its sword, this time making ready to stab at the crocodiles' eyes.

Meljul, for his part, continued to shuffle unobtrusively along a stout branch, towards the heart of the largest tree. He knew that there would be no point in trying to deploy his bow until he was much more securely positioned, and that it would be direly difficult to take aim through the tangled branches, but he was not unduly worried about that. After all, there would be time to decide which sort of creature he might take aim at once his various adversaries had settled their own urgent dispute.

He lost count of the marching monsters long before they stopped emerging from the doorway, but it was obvious that they outnumbered the sum of both groups of his erstwhile enemies. In the long run, he knew, they might well turn out to be the more dangerous enemy—in which case, he supposed, it might make sense, absurd as it seemed, to put one or two of them down so that the Tuaregs and the skull-faces would stand a better chance of further reducing their number. He was extremely reluctant to do that, though;

for the time being, it seemed wisest to watch and wait. Was it conceivable, he wondered, that the crocodiles might turn out not to be enemies at all? Was it possible that they might be capable of gratitude, were he to shoot down a few Tuaregs to help them out? There was no way to tell, as yet.

In the meantime, the skull-face with the slender sword had crouched down, and was already reaching out with the sharp point of its weapon—but the crocodiles cringed away from the blade, and proved surprisingly clever in moving their heads to avoid the blade. The Tuaregs, having got up high enough to be out of reach while the crocodiles still had their feet on the floor, were now ready to resume hurling every missile they could lay their hands on at their new adversaries, who were forming a ragged arc and closing in on the tree in which they had taken refuge.

At least six of the crocodiles were struck by arrows or flying daggers within a matter of seconds, but they seemed quite untroubled by the blows. There did not seem to be any blood flowing from the wounds, and not one of them had stumbled. Their progress was measured but inexorable.

By the time Meljul had contrived to reach a situation that satisfied him fully, perched on the broad back of one of the more batrachian idols, where he was hidden from both the altar and the gap in the roof by barriers of leafy branches, the vanguard of the second party of Tuaregs and skull-faces had reached the top of the ramp outside the temple wall. They could see what was happening well enough, but they were in no hurry to interfere. Meljul suspected that the bonds of loyalty existing between the Tuaregs and their allies were exceedingly weak, and that those linking the Tuaregs together with one another were far from unbreakable. For the moment, the newcomers were content to peer in and watch; they showed no great enthusiasm to rush to the aid of their four beleaguered companions.

Not one of the Tuaregs down below had been struck down as yet, but that was because the upright crocodilians had relatively short "arms" and carried no weapons. They were showing their teeth now, snapping at the heels of their tormentors, but they seemed to be doing so more by way of tokenistic intimidation rather than actual murderous intent. The skull-face had by far the longest reach of any of their opponents, but it had no intention of getting down from the altar, and while it remained there it was not difficult for the crocodiles to avoid the thrusts of its weapon. For a moment or two, the whole situation seemed to Meljul to be a mere dance, whose attempted violence had become merely theatrical.

The Tuaregs, however, were finding it harder to climb up the trees than it had been to climb down in the first place, and the older, desiccated branches were splintering in their hands or under foot. They had wasted too much time inflicting ineffectual wounds on their enemies, and haste was making them careless. One fell down as the branch on which he attempted to support himself gave way. Four crocodiles moved with unexpected alacrity to encircle him, and they ripped him apart, literally tearing his head off. By way of compensation, though, one of the four—which had an arrow embedded in its throat and a dagger buried to the hilt in its flank—suddenly collapsed, apparently having reached the limit of its unnaturally-sustained resilience.

As if that were a signal, the figures grouped around the gap under the eaves immediately began to fire arrows downwards, and to supplement the trickle of arrows with a more substantial rain of stones appropriated from the ramp or from the edges of the gap. However adept the crocodiles were at moving their heads to avoid sword-thrusts, they were too ungainly to dance out of the way of missiles falling from above. Another went down—and by now, Meljul judged, most of them must have suffered at least one damaging blow. On the other hand, a second Tuareg tumbled out of the tree, perhaps unexpectedly stuck from behind by friendly fire, and was swiftly dismembered.

To make matters worse for the initial invaders, the skull-face on the altar finally over-reached in one of its thrusts, and a crocodile grabbed his wrist. The skull-face was summarily pulled down from its perch, and it too was torn apart. That one, Meljul felt absolutely certain, would not be rising from the dead a second time.

Meljul counted up these casualties, and swiftly reached the conclusion that the battle was over. The only Tuareg left in the tree had now succeeded in climbing to a level from which it would be easy to reach the window. The missiles were still raining down, but the

Arab could not believe that anyone else would dare to come into the temple. The surviving Tuaregs and skull-faces had no alternative now but to retreat, no matter how much they might regret the loss of the scepter.

Provided that the crocodiles did not detect his presence, Meljul figured that he might be able to remain in hiding until both parties had gone their separate ways, leaving him to make his own retreat. He would not now have the advantage of a camel to ride, but it was possible that his horses were still waiting for him, and that he might be able to get access to the well again soon enough. With that thought in mind, the Arab relaxed his position, and put out a hand to grasp a bough in order to support himself a little better. Then he froze, trying with all his might to be as still as the statue on which he was squatting.

While he had been biding his time, a little snake had coiled itself around the bough that he had just grasped, and another had contrived to wind itself around another branch immediately above his head. Each snake had reacted to his slight but sudden displacement by setting its mouth threateningly agape, showing needle-sharp fangs moistened by the gleam of some viscous secretion.

Meljul had time to take note of the fact that each snake had two little horns on its head, above the eyes. The Arab had never actually encountered a horned viper in the flesh, and he was slightly surprised not to have found them much larger, but he was not deluded enough to think that their small size would make their venom any less deadly. Suddenly, the dense network of branches that surrounded him seemed not at all protective, and horribly unsafe.

Neither snake struck at him immediately, and he considered himself fortunate on that score—doubly fortunate, perhaps, in that he could see no more of their kin in the branches above his head—but he knew that he had to move to a clearer space as soon as he could, without provoking a strike, and that he had to be far more vigilant in future, if he were fortunate enough to be able to execute the maneuver.

He looked around for the most suitable location, hardly taking any notice of the crocodiles, which were now moving back to avoid being struck by miscellaneous projectiles.

The fight's over, he thought. *If I can just make myself safe….*

He was wrong. Perhaps the skull-faces had taken encouragement from the crocodiles' retreat, or perhaps they simply had a stronger impulse to vengeance than the Tuaregs, but they were no longer waiting at the top of the ramp. Before the last Tuareg had a chance to complete his climb and make his exit, five skull-faces came in through the breach, and began climbing down to the temple floor. One of them, Meljul knew, had to be the one that he had already "killed", but he had removed the arrow that had earlier been protruding from the stubborn creature's back, and it must have recovered from the wound; none of the five now seemed conspicuously less agile than the other four.

Better and better, Meljul told himself, although there was a measurer of desperation in his insistence. *If I can just get far enough away from the accursed vipers, my enemies outside will be reduced in number to four. A good bowman can surely pick off four frightened Tuaregs, if my friends the crocodiles can take care of the five skull-faces for me.*

He succeeded in moving away from the snakes without either of them striking at his arm or his face, and any evidence he gave of his movement surely passed unnoticed amid the hectic rustling that preceded the skull-faces arrival in the arena of combat. All five were wielding swords, and all five looked as if they had some skill in fencing. They wasted no time before attacking the huddled crocodiles. They inflicted cut after cut—but all to no avail, or so it seemed. The crocodiles would not bleed any more than the skull-faces did, neither did they fall.

As Meljul settled into a new place of refuge, he observed that the Tuaregs in the roof-cavity were at least prepared to provide their comrades with supporting fire. Two of them continued firing arrows, while the other two—including the climber, who had now reached the gap were busy hacking at the crumbling fabric of the roof, breaking loose missiles to throw. It was, in all probability, neither bravery nor loyalty that was inspiring them, Meljul realized, but the greed that had ensnared their companions. They were trying to even the odds, because they hoped that the last survivor of the conflict might yet obtain a clear run at the scepter—whose multi-colored glow now seemed greatly intensified to Meljul, although that might have been an illusion.

The Arab's new place of apparent safety was close to one of the eight walls of the temple, a considerable distance away from the face containing the gap through which he and the other outsiders had gained entrance. There were plenty of branches nearby, but they were all dead and desiccated, offering no useful cover even to subtle serpents. He had a clearer view from there of the open space before and beyond the altar, and of the conflict that raged there.

At long last, the crocodilian monsters were now able to bring their forepaws fully into play against enemies on the ground, but they had neither fingers nor opposable thumbs, so their "hands" were exceedingly clumsy, and their blunt claws were no use for stabbing or tearing. They managed to strike the swords from two of the skull-faces' hands, but they had not yet inflicted a mortal wound on any of their new opponents. At last, though, one of the five skull-faces was seized by one of the crocodiles, in what might have seemed in other circumstances to be a loving hug. It was held tightly, but it was not dismembered as its predecessor had been. No matter how extravagantly the skull-face wriggled, it could not get free.

Then a second skull-face was seized, and a third. Like parents restraining unruly children, the creatures that held them quelled their struggles determinedly—but in a conspicuously gentle fashion that contrasted sharply with their handling of earlier captives. The remaining two still had their swords, but all their judicious thrusting had not yet succeeded in bringing another crocodile down; both gave up the fight and retreated. They were not pursued; the crocodiles that were still unburdened turned away from their kin, but only to take up defensive positions. One of them did fall, then, but it was too late to make any difference to the decision to retreat.

The three skull-faces that had been taken captive began shouting at their retreating companions, but Meljul could not understand the language they used, and he had no idea whether they were shouting for help or offering advice. Meljul realized, not quite as gladly as he might have anticipated, that the two snakes that had threatened him might well have been adopting the same attitude to him as the crocodiles were now offering to the two retreating skull-faces and the Tuaregs beneath the roof. They had not even tried to strike at him; perhaps their only purpose had been to make him move away and let them alone. But what did the crocodiles want with their three captives?

There was, of course, a sacrificial altar here—and perhaps there was also a priest with a sacrificial knife, who was yet to emerge from the darkness—but could individuals who had already died once count as human sacrifices a second time around? Meljul could not restrain a slight smile as he imagined the amazement of the hypothetical priest on discovering that his intended victims were no longer capable of shedding blood. On the other hand, he thought, the crocodiles might be fully aware of the fact that their present opponents were not to be numbered among the truly living, having captured them in order to make a truce with them—a truce whose terms might bode ill for the living.

Throughout his life, Ahmad Meljul had always laughed at superstitious men who were so fearful of evil magic that they took ominous delight in proclaiming that there were fates even worse than death, of which murder was the merest part. Now, for the first time, he wondered whether they might be right. What on Earth was happening here? What were the skull-faces and the crocodiles trying to accomplish, and how, exactly, had they come into conflict? Might it all turn out, in the end, to be some sort of misunderstanding? Might the two sets of monsters decide, in the end, to band together against the avaricious humans who were the temple's true desecrators?

This place, Meljul realized, was surely a baited trap. Its treasure was intact because it was far too well-guarded to be taken away, but it remained on display as a lure, whose purpose was to tempt thieves and soldiers of fortune. He and the Tuaregs, not the skull-faces, had been the intended victims of the trap, and the crocodiles probably knew that. Now that they had taken most of the skull-faces out of the fight, they were free to redirect their attention to their real quarry. The Arab knew that he was still in imminent mortal danger, and virtually helpless.

But this is not an inescapable trap, he told himself. *Others have been in it, and returned to tell the tale.* As soon as he formed the thought, though, he guessed that Étienne Marin, or whoever had originated the tale that Marin had appropriated, had probably not *escaped* at all, even though the person in question had found his way back to civilization. The greater probability was that he had merely been appointed to serve as better and further-reaching bait: more effective bait than the glowing scepter itself.

9.

Edmond Kerval had no difficulty at all making his way back to the temple, now that he could see perfectly well even in the deepest darkness. Nor had he any fear of so doing, given that the crocodiles had not made the slightest move against him. He did not suppose that the Tuaregs posed any further danger to him now, even if there were six of them waiting without, with six skull-faces to back them up. Even so, when he came to the doorway he hung back, content to remain hidden in the shadows while he watched the progress of the battle.

He watched the crocodiles close in with mechanical efficiency upon their prey, seemingly not caring in the least whether their underbellies were stabbed and slashed. He took note of the fact that they did not seem to be acting as independent individuals, but rather as components of the same intelligence. He deduced from this observation that they were not really alive at all, but were merely pawns of his new master's guiding intelligence. Perhaps they had been actual crocodiles not long ago, or perhaps they had been placed in a state of suspended animation in the distant past, when the evil godling to whom this temple had been erected had still been the subject of active worship, and carefully stored away to await the distant day when that worship might be revived.

He laughed when he thought that, and was surprised at himself—until he guessed that the laugh had not been his. He realized, too—and perhaps the realization was no more his than the laugh— that the temple had always been a fraud: a kind of joke as well as a ploy in the games that the djinn of old had delighted to play. The fact that it had continued to do its work throughout the long interval since Azazel had stolen a march on his demon kin was merely an extra twist to the joke.

I know what you are now, Kerval said, silently, as he saw the weapons removed, with clinical efficiency, from the hands of the captive skull-faces. *You are pawns, like the crocodiles, perhaps recently reanimated and perhaps brought out of long storage, but pieces in a game, whichever is the case. Plainly, though, you are instruments of a different player, manifestations of a different jest. Is your master friend or foe, potentially speaking?*

The skull-faces obviously had not known what kind of battle they were fighting, and were still uncertain. They had not known how to fight it, either; they had wasted their thrusts by aiming for the heart, the throat and the intestines of their reptilian adversaries, realizing far too late that none of those anatomical elements were necessary to the movement or the nature of the imitation crocodiles.

Kerval knew that he was a playing-piece himself now, and might a well be grateful that he was no mere brutal pawn. Ahmad Meljul had told him more than once that all human roads led, in the ultimate analysis, to damnation, and he had always been prepared to concede the point. If, as certainly seemed to be the case, he was now embarked upon one that was more precipitous than the rest, he must do his best to keep his feet and enjoy the journey. With luck, it might prove to be a scenic route, and one that was not entirely deprived of luxury.

The captive skull-faces were calling out urgently to their retreating companions, and to the Tuaregs huddled around the gap high up in the wall—a gap, Kerval observed, that was now much wider than it had been when he first saw it. He knew that they were hoping for rescue, or at least distant assistance, but he could see that their pleas were going unanswered. The rain of missiles from above slowed, and then stopped. There was a general pause, as if everyone present were curious to know what the crocodiles intended to do with their captives.

The crocodiles that were still standing—only two had been struck down—took advantage of the pause to inspect their wounds. None was bleeding copiously, but three or four began to sag visibly now that they were no longer moving purposefully. One seemed to have been blinded.

Kerval counted the survivors up above, and reckoned the total as two skull-faces and three Tuaregs. All five were now massed in the gap beneath the eaves. *Well,* he thought, *at least Ahmad Meljul is safe. There is no one guarding the well now, so he will be free to slake his thirst before making his escape. I wish you well, my friend.*

"Don't be so eager to bid your friend goodbye," a tiny but perfectly audible voice in his inner ear instructed him. "Whatever progress there has been while I was not here to observe, I dare say that the great majority of men are what they always were: great fools or little ones. If your friend is hereabouts, you'll see him again."

He's a useful man to have on your side, Kerval was quick to say, silently. *Treat him gently, and he'll be as good a servant to you as I will.* Then he laughed softly—except, once again, that he was not the one who was amused.

Kerval knew that he had already bartered his soul, and was not in any position to make demands of his new master. He also knew that it would be wise not to offend his possessor—but he was in no position to keep secrets. He had to hope that his protector might be the kind of god who would not only grant his subjects the right to form opinions, but might be able to respect and admire a measure of imaginative daring. Instead of merely having the temerity to wonder how a company of entities as seemingly powerful as the djinn of the Land of the Dead could have been so careless as to allow an entire nation of worshippers to vanish from the face of the Earth, therefore, Kerval let his imagination roam, questing for an explanation.

If I were an idle godling, he thought, *with incalculable power and potentially-eternal existence, my greatest enemy would be boredom. If I were inclined to wrath, I might take the edge off that boredom with never-ending orgies of violence. If I were inclined to intellectual ambition, I might become a creator and solver of intricate puzzles and bizarre games. If I were inclined to lust and luxury, I would surely dedicate myself to sensual self-indulgence. When I had run the gamut of sensation, though, I would always be vulnerable to the bittern dullness of satiation—and I would be prudent, in my own fashion. Although I would have no option but to revert to the state of boredom, again and again and again, only able to distract myself for a little while, I would be very careful to put my toys away with the utmost care, in order that I might keep a vast storehouse of instruments of amusement, any one of which might have regained its potential for amusement during the long years, centuries or millennia of its neglect. Satiation is, after all, a temporary thing, even for men. Hunger, thirst and lust, no matter how successfully they are appeased, always return; every appetite fed is an appetite that will be renewed in the fullness of time. So it must be for demons, of whose appetites our human appetites are but feeble reflections. This city has evidently served its interval of neglect, and is ready to be born again—in which case, I have an opportunity to be far more than a petty pawn, or even a tame magician. I might yet be a veritable redeemer!*

This time, when Kerval laughed, he was laughing for himself—but he was hoping that another might join in, and share his hopes while sharing his joke.

Instead, he stepped forward from the doorway into open, and drew himself up to his full height, in order that he might seem as imposing as possible, in spite of his ragged state. He marched forward, so that everyone could see him: not merely the crocodiles and their captives, but also the anxious watchers outside the wall. It was the latter—or, at least, the skull-faces among them—to whom he turned first, and to whom he raised his arm, in a gesture that was half-placatory and half-menacing, but when he began speaking he was talking to the captive company as well.

"There is no need to fight," he said, although he said it in a language that was not his own, and would not have understood the day before. "We have been rivals before, and our armies have clashed in glorious combat, but we have a common enemy now, who must be hunted down, tried, and punished severely before we put our minds to any other purpose. The Land of the Dead must be reshaped as well as reborn, with a new political order. You came here to steal, I know, and I do not resent the attempt—but that opportunity is gone, and there is a greater reward to be obtained: an alliance of Semiaza and Jeqon, against the vile deceiver Azazel. Nor will that be the limit of the alliance, for the first move in the new game must be its expansion to include the others that were bound and narcotized—as many, at least, as can be freed or woken up."

There was a moment's hesitation before the reply came, but one of the two skull-faces up above took the initiative soon enough.

"You're too late to play the master this time, Semiaza," the skull-face said. "*Our* alliance is already made—and if you want to join it, you'll have to pay a price."

Kerval felt an astonishing surge of anger—astonishing even though he knew full well that it was not his. His hand was still raised, and it hardly moved—but the gesture it was making no longer had any placatory element in it; it was all menace now.

"You're on my ground, you fools!" he said—and his index-finger was suddenly extended, with an abrupt stabbing motion aimed at the gap in which the two skull-faces and three Tuaregs were standing.

The wall supporting the five creatures crumbled, and they fell.

Having had no intention himself, let alone the power to actualize his intention, Kerval could not quite believe, for a moment or two, that the collapse was anything more than an accident—an inevitable accident, given that the wall must have been severely weakened by the damage inflicted upon it in the last hour, but an accident nevertheless. *But what is demonic power, after all*, he told himself, *if not the ability to command nature's accidents?*

The three Tuaregs and their skull-face companions tumbled down as if in slow motion, clutching desperately at the tree-branches that interrupted their fall—but those branches had been damaged too, by previous descents and the multitudinous missiles hurled down from the breach. All five of them fell all the way to the floor, and made a very solid impact as they met its dislocated tiles. Kerval imagined that he could actually hear limbs breaking.

Those crocodiles that were not yet holding prisoners, and were still capable of fluent movement, moved forward as if to pick up the fallen bodies—but their intended victims were not quite done for yet. The one Tuareg that did not make any attempt to scramble out of the way was tossed aside as soon as he had been picked up, dead or unconscious. Both the skull-faces rose to their feet, somewhat unsteadily, with blades in their hands. The other Tuaregs were both expressing their distress in gasps and grimaces of pain, but they both contrived to rise to their feet, ready to face the crocodiles.

The crocodiles paused.

Kerval bent down to pick up a brace of discarded weapons: a scimitar and a mace. The single-edged sword was cruder than his own saber and quite differently weighted, but he was confident that he could wield it effectively, even without demonic aid. He had never wielded a mace, always considering such weapons far too brutal for a gentleman's use, but he had picked the weapon up in preference to a javelin that lay nearby because he thought it would be more useful in hand-to-hand combat. He moved smoothly to support the lumbering crocodiles, quite ready to make use of his greater agility in leading the attack.

The Tuaregs must have been astonished by his presence, let alone his actions, but that did not make them any less determined to take him on, and the way they met his stare suggested that they were determined to make him their primary target, so resentful were they of his involvement in the affair. As soon as he moved to engage them they were quick to retaliate, thrusting at him in unison.

The Breton parried their blades with his own, and thumped one over the head with the mace before either of them had time to organize another thrust. When the second thrust came from the one still standing he met it with the shaft of the mace, and smashed the blunt side of his sword-blade into the side of the Tuareg's head. That one went down too, similarly stunned, but not yet dead.

The crocodiles gathered both of them in.

The taller of the two skull-faces immediately broke off its engagement with the crocodiles to rush Kerval, but never reached him. The crocodile from which he turned away lifted up one of its feet and swept its tail along the floor to trip the skull-face, which fell with unexpected heaviness. The other immediately moved to support it, presumably intending to win it time to regain its feet, but the fallen skull-face suddenly let out a most unexpected howl of anguish and raised its slender arm as if in panic. Kerval saw that there was a little snake dangling from the forearm, in which the serpent's fangs were firmly embedded.

Caught between natural life and death as it might be, the skull-face was evidently not immune to viper venom. The creature writhed madly for a moment or two, and then collapsed, seemingly paralyzed. Its last remaining companion had frozen in shock when it heard the unprecedented howl of pain, and it too was promptly struck by a second snake, equally tiny, which sank its fangs into the creature's ankle. The skull-face remained standing for a few seconds more, and then collapsed.

Crocodiles picked up both bodies.

The vipers must have been disturbed when the bodies fell from above, Kerval thought, *and maddened with alarm—but that is demonic power, is it not? Snakes have always been allied with demons, and these must know their master.*

The fight was over now; every Tuareg who was still alive, and every skull-face, had now been seized and imprisoned by Semiaza's minions. Kerval looked around, without knowing, at first, what he was looking for—but then he figured it out.

What he wanted—needed—was a blade much shorter and sharper than the one he presently held: the kind of blade that might be used in offering up a human sacrifice on an altar built for that purpose.

10.

Ahmad Meljul watched in fascination as his former friend—who had now revealed an altogether inexplicable knowledge of an alien language—took up a position behind the altar, while a crocodile brought a mewling Tuareg captive towards the sacrificial block.

Kerval seemed to be in a parlous state—as might be expected of a man who had fallen down a well—but he was moving with an alarmingly mechanical sense of purpose. His clothes were in tatters, and he seemed to be carrying at least a dozen superficial but bloody wounds, but he was not showing the slightest sign of discomfort, distress or uncertainty. On the contrary: his eyes were gleaming with a fervor that could not be entirely explained by the fact that the surrounding area was bathed in the light of sunbeams flooding through the damaged roof and the colored light of the glowing scepter.

It seemed to Meljul that there was a peculiar redness in the gleam in Kerval's eyes, far more profound than could be expected, even allowing for the fact that they were been reflecting the eerie glow of the scepter as well as the glare of the sun.

Meljul's first response, on seeing his companion alive, had been a surge of delight, but now that he had seen the way in which Kerval had stunned the two Tuaregs he was no longer sure that he had any reason to be delighted. Whatever miracle had preserved the Breton's life seemed also to have transformed him into an agent of the idol. Meljul had always been too cautious to believe that his Breton friend could be entirely trusted; it seemed safer now to proceed on the assumption that he could not be trusted at all. So the Arabian remained hidden in the shadows, watching carefully to see what would happen next.

The reptilian monster that had come forward to the altar placed its terrified captive on the concave surface, without letting go of the Tuareg's arms. The crocodile's forepaws made rather inefficient hands, but once they had a grip they were certainly capable of maintaining it. The creature had been cut in a dozen places, but it had not released a single drop of blood and its muscular strength seemed undiminished. It carefully changed its grip so as to hold the man down, stretched out in a supine position.

Edmond Kerval cut the Tuareg's throat, and stood over his victim, as if mesmerized, watching arterial blood rise up in a fountain before falling back into the shallow bowl. Meljul knew that the blood must be red, but it was dark enough to seem almost black in the still-uncertain light. While it gushed forth extravagantly, the black blood spattered the Breton's face and breast, but once the flood had slowed to a trickle, every drop drained into the concave surface of the altar.

Until this point in time, Meljul had not heard any of the crocodilian monsters emit the slightest sound—but now they sighed, in unison, opening their mouths wide to display unnaturally white teeth and sturdy grey tongues. Even the ones whose legs were hurt, so that they could no longer stand erect, and the one whose eyes had been put out, so that it could not see, joined in the sigh.

"My faithful servants," Kerval said, not only speaking with obvious theatricality but reverting to the Latin-based patois that served as the common language of Mediterranean merchandising—although Meljul was unconvinced that the crocodiles were capable of understanding it—"this is a new beginning. Tuareg blood is by no means rich and by no means sweet, but every great crusade must start with a single step. Blood is blood, after all—and had my host not shed a little of his own, voluntarily, into this same avid receptacle, we might have contrived nothing here today but a petty massacre—but I believe that we have done better than that." Then he made a curt gesture, whose meaning was unmistakable. The crocodiles sighed again when the Tuareg's body was hauled away and cast aside, all the blood having been wrung from its body by the monster's patient massage. This time, the victim brought forward was a skull-face—but the skull-faces, Meljul already knew, did not bleed.

Kerval did not seem to care. He cut the skull-faces throat, and then, when no fountain of blood gushed forth, cut off its head. Then he slit its belly, and spilled its intestines into the bowl.

He's mad, Meljul thought. *Completely mad—and who can blame him, if he's been keeping such company. He evidently believes himself to be a guest of the idol, obliged to pay for the hospitality he has received—but why haven't the crocodiles killed him? How on Earth has he contrived to befriend them?*

"No blood?" said Kerval, still speaking the same language that he had been forced to employ for the last two years of his life. "Well, no matter. The blood is only a symbol, after all—it slakes no thirst. I shall read the entrails, by way of divination of the future—that will be a useful ability, in times to come. I see the Land of the Dead reborn, and restored to its former glory—no, to a greater glory still. Whether we are capable of forming alliances or not, we shall carry the great quest forward alongside our petty squabbles—and this time, I think, we shall find opportunities for amusement and instruction that we never known. It seems that there has been progress in the world of men while we have been asleep, and that will add spice to our reborn empire. We shall need far more recruits to our cause, though, than the lure of the scepter can possibly provide. We must go out into the world of men, as Jeqon's minions have already done, to make what alliances we may and what conquests we can. The road will be long and hard, but we are ready for anything, are we not?"

The biped crocodiles made no reply—but they sighed again when the skull-face was replaced by the other Tuareg, who bled blackly, with astonishing generosity, while his stubborn heart refused to acknowledge death. Meljul could not see what was happening to the fraction of the man's blood that flowed into the shallow bowl, but it did not overspill the sides. The Arab could see well enough, though that Edmond Kerval had been liberally splashed, and that the red glow in the Breton's eyes seemed even more glaring in consequence.

If Kerval did not come here by the same route as the rest of us, Meljul thought, forcing himself to concentrate on practical matters, *there must be a passage of some kind connecting the bowels of the temple to the bottom of the well. If it is navigable in one direction, it must be navigable in the other. If the trees herein are infested with vipers, which have now been roused from their habitual somnolence, there is probably no safe way back to that yawning gap high up in the wall, but the dark doorway from which Kerval emerged would be easy enough to attain if there were fewer monsters in the way. What I need is a distraction that would give me time to make a run at it.*

While a fourth victim—another bloodless one—was brought to the altar, Meljul took stock of his remaining equipment. He still had Kerval's saber, but it was no use to him just now. Apart from his own dagger, his quiver of arrows and the water-skin he had stolen from a camel's back, the only other thing he had about his person was Kerval's pouch, whose exact contents he had not yet bothered to ascertain. As the crocodiles sighed yet again, Meljul took the pouch from his second belt and tipped out its contents, in order to ascertain the sum of Edmond Kerval's worldly goods.

The Breton's wealth consisted of an embroidered handkerchief, the key to a lock that was presumably more than six hundred leagues away, a device for extracting stones from horses' hooves, a mummified hare's foot, a small pair of scissors, a tangled ball of thread—but no accompanying needle—a spare belt-buckle, a screw of tobacco—but no pipe—a whetstone, an ill-made flintlock with a wispy hank of kindling-wool, a short length of twine and three brass rings which could be used for the attachment of various items of bridle and harness.

Ahmad Meljul was a simple man, who did not believe in carrying overmuch clutter, but he was suddenly glad that Edmond Kerval took a more civilized view of the accumulation of personal possessions. "If I get out of this alive," he muttered, "I'll never laugh at another effete European, no matter how many of them I might have to murder in the natural course of my projects." So saying, he took up the flintlock and the kindling-wool, and then moved sideways until he was in close proximity to a substantial aggregation of ancient branches, which had been dead and dry for hundreds of years.

He struck a spark, which immediately set the kindling-wool alight—and when he set the kindling-wool among the branches, they caught fire with amazing alacrity. It was as if they had been as hungry for fire as the altar had apparently been for the blood of the living and the entrails of the dead.

Meljul retreated from the gathering blaze with all due expedition, making his way swiftly to an empty angle of the octagonal temple, which was almost as distant from the cramped and twisted foliage of the ancient trees as its opposite, where the dark doorway was. There were two possible routes to that doorway from where Meljul now crouched, neither of them quite straight. He could go to the left of the altar or to the right. There was far more space to the right, but that area was still crowded with emburdened crocodiles; behind the altar there was, for the moment, no one but Edmond Kerval—who might well have moved out of the way by the time Meljul made his dash, and might not be inclined to stop him even if he had not. While Meljul made ready to run, the fire made rapid headway.

Not one of the six trees that had taken root in the temple's interior had been growing for significantly less than a thousand years. Each one had fought long and hard for every drop of water its questing roots had dragged from the stony earth below. Their patterns of growth had been built into their seeds, and they had had no alternative but to put forth branches in every direction, even though the branches that could not find sunbeams to nourish them had withered and died in consequence. Trees have no eyes with which to see, and no minds with which to plan, so they had continued putting out new branches wherever there was space, even when there was no possibility that they would ever find a ray of light to bring forth leaves from their living heart. In their own strange fashion, therefore, those long-dead branches *were* as avid for fire as the evil altar was for blood. The fire leapt from one to another with an appetite that would have been incredible in a man, perhaps even in a djinni.

White smoke billowed out in churning clouds, but could not choke the flames, which hurled themselves upwards and outwards: towards the roof-space filled with warm and moistureless air, and towards the gaps where more air could be sucked out of the desert sky. The gaps were not easy to reach, because of the living and leafy wood that clustered about them, but the fire was burning hotter with every second that elapsed, and nothing could stand in its way.

The crocodiles, Meljul supposed, could not be dead and dry, for they had surely come into the temple by the same river-road as Kerval. Even so, the stricken ones that were stretched out horizontally were close enough to the woody litter that littered the floor beneath the trees to be caught in the sudden rush of fire that swept across the paving-stones; they did not burn, but they were roasted. Blades had not been able to hurt the creatures overmuch, but burning evidently did. The crocodiles that were still standing erect retreated from the flames in terror, although they were too stubborn to release their iron grip upon their scaly captives.

The skull-faces did not seem to like fire any more than the crocodiles did; the remaining captives had been sullenly silent while they waited churlishly to be sliced up by Kerval's knife, but they now began to scream. Meljul had always thought of living human beings as good screamers, but he had never had an adequate opportunity to weigh up the potential opposition. He wasted no time now in conceding now, privately, that the dead—or the undead—were very good screamers indeed.

It was obvious now that Meljul could not remain where he was for a second longer, else there would be nothing left for him to breathe in the smoke-filled air. He had to make his move, and did so. He began his dash with a blade in each hand, hoping that Edmond Kerval would have sense enough not to get in his way—and perhaps even sense enough to abandon his recently-discovered vocation as a mad high-priest of an abandoned idol, and revert to his former career as an honest thief and plunderer.

11.

In all his twenty-three years of life, Edmond Kerval had never felt better than he did when he plunged his borrowed dagger into the flesh of the first Tuareg sacrifice. The good feeling began *before* the first drop of arterial blood touched his skin, but there seemed nothing strange in that. Common men, as he knew only too well, found it easy enough to distinguish between anticipation and fulfillment, but he was no longer a common man. Demons, he presumed, had sufficient will-power to alloy intention and reward into a perfect whole—and this facility had to be one of the echoes that resonated in the souls of the possessed.

The Breton was hardly conscious of making his florid speech, which was not really directed at the crocodiles, but merely at himself, by way of clarification and consolation. He did not feel the blood raining upon his face even when the second Tuareg was offered to him, because the blood already seemed to be a part of him. He did not thirst for it because he did not need to; it had already undergone whatever process of digestion had been necessary to convert it into the fabric of his own mysterious being. It seemed to him that the tattered remnants of his shirt did not become soaked, because the sacrificial blood—no longer bound by the common laws of fluid dynamics—passed right through the material and into his breast.

Edmond Kerval felt *wonderful*, and knew that it was, indeed, because he was full of wonders. He had, of course, to suppose that they were *evil* wonders, but he had never made any conspicuous efforts to be a good man, and his only regret was that he had wasted twenty-three years before finding a useful opportunity to embrace evil as it needed to be embraced. He knew now how trivial the record of his own petty thefts, frauds and treasons had been.

He knew, now, the luxury of reckless violence and whole-hearted self-indulgence.

One intriguing side-effect of his new-found inability to distinguish anticipation from fulfillment was that he had become incapable of surprise. Events could no longer astonish him, even when they were authentically unexpected and inconvenient. He was above annoyance now, and beyond fear—so when the fire leapt up, like a berserk giant, to consume the paradoxical trees that were more dead than alive, the questions that snaked sluggishly into his mind were quite casual, even though they contained a measure of wonderment at the quirky ways of fate.

Did I request a holocaust? he asked, flippantly. *Do I require an orgy of conflagration to add to my other delights? Is this really necessary to the renewal of my long-dormant amusement? Do I care, one way or the other?*

Kerval watched, more bewildered than irritated, as the recumbent crocodiles perished in the flames and the remainder retreated in panic. The excessive heat of the petty forest's rapid combustion caused the flesh and blood of the various corpses lying beneath the flames to boil, and then to degrade into odorous black tar. The space behind the altar filled up with cloying smoke, but the clouds could not obscure Kerval's newly-augmented power of vision, and his blood-nourished lungs drank in the particles without difficulty, as if they were a piquant spice lightly sprinkled on the healthful air.

Something came hurtling out of the shadows to the right of the altar then: something seemingly blind and mad, presumably impelled by a reckless alloy of panic and determination. The thing had two arms and two legs, but it was too long-limbed to be a crocodile and not slender enough to be a skull-face. It carried a blade in each hand, one of which bore an uncanny resemblance to a saber that had one been Kerval's most prized possession, but neither hand made any attempt to cut him down. The racing form seemed quite content to knock him out of the way so that it could run past, heading into the shadows on the opposite side of the altar.

A human, obviously, Kerval thought, as he landed flat on his back, feeling neither jarred nor bruised, nor even unjustly insulted by the tumble. *What else is human life but a blind flight from one shadow to another, impelled by helpless panic and mistaken deter-mination, supported by borrowed weapons in whose use one is woe-fully inexpert?* When Kerval rose to his feet again, though, he re-membered that even humans were not *complete* fools. Sometimes, there were good reasons why they had to fly madly from shadow to shadow, and adequate intellectual justification for their insane hope that the shadows towards which they fled might contain a safer exit than those they had forsaken. Sometimes—for example, when a temple roof began to fall—there were good reasons why even the host of a demon of luxury and wrath might forsake the altar upon which he had been recently reborn, and equally good reasons for the hope that there might be a kind of safety to be found in mundane shadows.

Kerval had to suppose, as he looked up at the falling roof, that only a miracle of sorts had kept it so long from collapse. It must have been considerably weakened by the passage of the centuries—and it was, after all, an item of human manufacture, however demonically-inspired. Nothing built by humans could last forever; the miracle was that any such item lasted any time at all. The com-bined efforts of the Tuaregs and skull-faces, feverishly determined to widen the makeshift entrance so that they could follow their dreams or their kin, augmented by his own casual carelessness in causing the remainder to fall, had obviously brought the whole of the ancient roof to the very limit of its endurance—and the unlooked-for holocaust that had so rudely interrupted his sacrificial ritual had administered the *coup-de-grace.*

So the roof was falling, now.

Perhaps, Kerval thought, *I ought to get out of the way.*

Ordinarily, it would not have been the kind of decision that war-ranted careful consideration or in-depth discussion, but the Breton did not move immediately. He formed the intention to move, but intention was still strangely entwined in his consciousness with ful-fillment, so he felt—oddly enough—that he had *already* moved.

He also felt—perhaps even more oddly—that there was some-thing else that had yet to happen *before* he moved.

So he waited, and watched the stony fabric of the roof disintegrate as it fell, like a thunder-cloud turning precipitately to rain and hail.

He watched modestly-sized blocks descend upon the statues that stood in the gaps in the crumbling colonnade, smashing their ugly heads and misshapen bodies. He saw other blocks, of an altogether immoderate magnitude, descend upon the huge idol which loomed above him still, pulverizing its head and breaking both its arms—including, of course, the one that held the gem-encrusted scepter.

When the severed forearm hit the stone floor the hand shattered into a thousand shards—but the jade scepter rolled away, seemingly immune to all injury.

Edmond Kerval walked calmly away from his station behind the altar, ignoring the lumps of stone that were bursting like bombs as they hit the unforgiving floor on every side. He picked up the scepter, and rested the glowing head on his right shoulder. Then—and only then—he marched, with military precision, into the dust-shrouded shadows that concealed the doorway to the underworld.

12.

Ahmad Meljul had fallen twice in the pitch-black corridors, and had rapped his knuckles a dozen times against invisible and unforgiving walls, but he had kept on running, relentlessly, and he had refused to drop either of his blades in order to liberate his fingers.

Had it not been for the fire he had set, the Arab might have become irredeemably lost, but the fire was so fiercely avid for air that it sucked a considerable wind from the underworld beneath the temple, and all that he had to do was keep his face to that wind. That was not a hard thing to ask of himself, given that the wind was so cool, so clean and so moist.

In the end, the draught brought him to the flight of steps up which Edmond Kerval had climbed in the wake of his misadventure in the well. Meljul might have stumbled on the steps, bruising himself badly as he tumbled into the water, but luck was with him. Although he could not see anything at all, he was able to set his blades safely down beside him, within easy reach. He seated himself on a step with only his booted feet in the water, so that he could scoop up water in his cupped hands and pour it gratefully upon his head.

He drank a little, but only a little—he had no wish to make himself sick.

He lost track of time while he sat there, exhaustedly, but he was unconcerned by the loss. Time did not seem to have been on his side in the last few days, and he was not displeased to have an opportunity to set its corrosions aside for a while. Perhaps, he thought, it was kind of time's presiding djinn to let him do that—or perhaps the concession was merely one more trap, intended to catch and torment him. Either way, he did not look up again until his eyes were stimulated by light. As soon as the red gleam appeared, however, Meljul was seized by a sudden anxiety that he might have lingered too long, and would have done better to have plunged himself into the subterranean river immediately, no matter how desperate a move it had seemed.

The red light showed him the bare space that he had crossed in order to get to where he was, but it also showed him the walls that slanted towards the aperture from which he had emerged. The walls were covered in fungus and strange dark-blooming flowers, whose blossoms were nests for scorpions the size of his hand. The scorpions seemed to be prey, in their turn, to the kinds of leeches that preferred insectile ichor to vertebrate blood.

No part of this revelation could or would have frightened him, had it not been for the eerie quality of the red radiation that illuminated and excited them—but there was something about the glow that not merely invited, but demanded, terror.

Meljul felt the beat of his alarmed heart increase, and felt that he was in mortal danger. It took three full minutes for him to realize that the light was coming from the scepter that had formerly been held by the idol in the temple: the scepter that had been adequately protected from theft for thousands of years, against all the odds, and had continued all the while to do its patient and peculiar work.

Edmond Kerval had it now.

The artifact must have been heavy, but Kerval seemed quite comfortable with its mass. The Breton was resting the glowing head of the device upon his shoulder, but Meljul doubted that he was do-ing so to obtain relief from its weight; it seemed to the Arab that Kerval simply wanted to keep the glow as close to his face as possi-ble, in order to maintain the light in his own glowing eyes.

"Ahmad Meljul, my friend," Kerval said, in a perfectly level tone. "It's good to see you again. Do you still have my sword and pouch?"

"Yes, I do," Meljul answered, rising slowly to his feet as he spoke and adjusting his stance so that he could face the newcomer squarely. "The blade is as sharp as it ever was, but the pouch is a little lighter. I fear that your supply of kindling-wool is quite ex-hausted. I had need of it."

"No matter," Kerval said, casually. "We are partners in this en-terprise, after all. We must pool our resources as well as our re-wards, if we are to play the game as it needs to be played. Azazel will not be defeated in a day, and Jeqon has proved a sad disap-pointment. Perhaps he was one of those unfortunates sealed in a bot-tle, who went mad while he lay at the bottom of the sea."

Meljul was extremely surprised by this remarkable statement, but he was wary of expressing his surprise, having already real-ized—demonstrating his intellectual prowess once again—that Ed-mond Kerval was quite mad. The Arab knew that madmen had to be humored, or, at least, not annoyed. In any case, he was responsible for the poor fool, having drawn him into this adventure by commit-ting murder.

"You're absolutely right, my friend," Meljul said. "We must pool our resources as well as our rewards. How many gems are in that scepter's head do you think, and what might they be worth?—remembering of course, that our old adversaries, the merchants, will be determined to cheat us when we sell them."

"They're of no great value in coin, I fear," Kerval said, negli-gently. "We could not sell them, in any case, for they have a prop-erty that is far more useful to us than mere money."

"And what is that?" Meljul asked.

"Seduction," Kerval replied. "We must use it cleverly, if we are to gain the greatest advantage from it—but you and I are exception-ally clever men, are we not? We are aristocrats of the mind, as well as the flesh, and our cleverness has been increased rather than diminished by the fact that we have fallen on hard times. Solomon, whom you call Suleiman, had a great reputation for wisdom, but he was living in primitive times. There has been progress since then, has there not? Imagine what you and I could have done with the magical support that Solomon had! Imagine what we shall be able to do with it, in our own more complicated world!"

Meljul began to appreciate the truth, then. He realized that the red glow in Kerval's eyes was not, after all, the reflection of the scepter's light or the fire of madness. He was careful not to frown. Carefully, he stooped to pick up Kerval's saber, taking hold of it by the blade so that he could extend it hilt-first to his companion.

Kerval accepted the offering, and then waited for Meljul to take off the belt, the sheath and the pouch that went with it. When Meljul tried to hand all of those things to him at once, though, the Breton raised his elbows to emphasize the fact that his hands were full. Then the other man turned his body slightly, using the gesture language to indicate that Meljul might loop the belt around his waist and fasten it, so that the saber could be safely sheathed.

Meljul knew that this would be the last moment of decision. If he intended to attack his former partner, he ought to do it now; it would be far more difficult to do it later. There did not seem to be any urgent necessity to carry out such an attack, but he could not help wondering to what he might be committing himself, if he accepted the resumption of their association.

The Arab hesitated. "It seemed to me," he said, "while I was watching your performance at the altar, that the blood of a sacrifice to an evil god might have stained you," he observed, mildly. "Indeed, I was almost persuaded by illusion that it passed into your flesh as you sacrificed the Tuaregs."

"I suppose I have been stained," Kerval admitted. "And I admit that there is something within me now that was not there before—but everything that I have accepted into my flesh and my soul was merely answering a thirst I already had—a thirst that all human beings have, although there are some who seem to take a perverse delight in their refusal to give way to it. We came here in search of enrichment, my friend, and we have found it. Are you unready, my dear Ahmad, after all we have suffered, to claim the entirety of your inheritance?"

"If you will pardon me for saying so, my dear Edmond," Meljul said, gently, "you have not seemed quite yourself since you fell into the well. I am not quite sure what to make of you just now."

"You are not required to make anything of me," Kerval countered. "I am a self-made man, as all proud Bretons of good family desire to be. The question is: what will you make of yourself?"

Meljul glanced around at the walls, which were still swarming with exotic vermin. He remembered that he had passed his hand along those walls, and had come away with nothing worse than the slime of crushed fungus upon them. The scorpions had refrained from stinging him, and the leeches had refrained from sucking his blood, just as the horned vipers in the temple had earlier refrained from biting him. That was not the nature of such creatures; they were evidently operating under some alien influence. Other men might have accounted that influence generous as well as kindly, but Ahmad Meljul was a man had followed the imperatives of his profession in ceasing to believe in kindness, let alone in generosity. He remembered the promise he had made in the desert, to give his loyalty to any djinn that might be disposed to take the trouble to save him. Perhaps this one had heard and perhaps it had not, but he had to make good on his promise either way. He was, after all, a man who took his responsibilities seriously.

"I have never had the slightest ambition to be a priest or a magician," Meljul said, calmly. He had not known that it was true until he said it, but it *was* true. He had not known that it was irrelevant until he said it, either, but it *was* irrelevant.

"If you were to attack me, my friend," Kerval pointed out, equably, "you would need to be very quick and exceedingly clever. Perhaps you could run me through before I could bash out your brains, and perhaps not. I think not, but you might disagree, so I shall not press the point; instead, let us look calmly at the possible outcomes. In one case, I would die and you would live; in another, you would die and I would live; in the third, we would both die. Consider only the first, which is the only one of three that you might reckon less than catastrophic. What would you do when I lay stretched upon the staircase, the scepter having tumbled from my hand? Would you pick it up, or leave it where it lay? Perhaps you would be a hero in the eyes of your fellow men if you were to kill me, and perhaps you would be a fool—but in either case, what would you become thereafter? What would you become, if you were to stand here all alone, with the scepter at your feet?"

Ahmad Meljul laughed. "A fair point," he conceded, "but an unnecessary one. I have not the slightest intention of attacking you, my friend, even though I can feel the scepter's seductive force. I am a murderer and a thief, but I am not a man who would betray a friend—even a friend who is not quite himself. The decision over which I am hesitating is merely a matter of whether to stay with you, now that you are mad or possessed, or both, or whether to go my own way."

The man with fire in his eyes blinked slowly, as if to prevent them from overheating. "I apologize, my friend," he said. "I am, as you say, not quite myself at present—but I'm a rapid learner. I shall deal with you as I tried, unsuccessfully, to deal with Jeqon's minions. I shall make you no promises, although I dare say that I could. I could certainly promise you wealth, power and luxury. I could probably promise you a share in an empire—and what is worth more than that, although you might not believe it: a share in all the joy and triumph of *building* an empire, of shaping its nature and future. I will not do that, though, for I am uncertain as yet as to what I might be able to achieve for myself in this newly-hatched world; what I will do instead is to offer you an opportunity to make *something* of yourself that is more than you are now, and better. As for the fee you must pay in return—well, I shall play the honest trader and admit to you that it is exceedingly high, although it may not be haggled down.

"Now you know all that you need to know, my friend, and you understand more than most men will ever be privileged to understand. So tell me, Ahmad Meljul: *what will you make of yourself?*"

Still Meljul hesitated, but he knew that the hesitation was no more now than mere prideful display. He already knew what he had to do, what he was, and what he was about to become. There was a sense in which he had known it since the moment immediately before the one in which he had turned in his saddle to put an arrow into the breast of one of the pursuing skull-faces, in order to win himself and Kerval a brief remission from the long pursuit. That was the moment when he had first realized that there was a road of sorts across the desert: a road as yet invisible to Edmond Kerval, but clear enough to a desert-bred man; a road that would lead them both to damnation.

Meljul had known as soon as he began to make out the ancient traces of that route that it was a road not to be followed lightly or carelessly—but he had also known that every road he had ever followed in his entire life, by land or by sea, had been directed to intersect with it. He understood, now, that he had already passed the crossroads of his own existence, and that only a perfectly human capacity for denial and self-delusion had kept him from knowing that the gap between anticipation and fulfillment is always an illusion of time and thought.

Ahmad Meljul placed the sword-belt around Edmond Kerval's waist, and buckled it for him.

Kerval sheathed his saber. "We have no time to waste, my friend," the Breton said. "We need to find a safe way out of here as soon as we can. This road has a great deal further to take us, and we had best be on our way. The djinn are returning to reclaim their heritage; there is toilsome work to be done, and a marvelous game to play."

"I'm sure that you are right, my friend," Meljul replied. "It will, I think, be a game worth playing—which is perhaps as well, given that it appears to be the only one that will accept us as players."

They went forth into the darkness then, comfortable in their friendship, guided by the red light and their own refreshed powers of sight.

ABOUT THE AUTHOR

BRIAN STABLEFORD was born in Yorkshire in 1948. He taught at the University of Reading for several years, but is now a full-time writer. He has written many science fiction and fantasy novels, including *The Empire of Fear*, *The Werewolves of London*, *Year Zero*, *The Curse of the Coral Bride*, and *The Stones of Camelot*. Collections of his short stories include *Sexual Chemistry: Sardonic Tales of the Genetic Revolution*, *Designer Genes: Tales of the Biotech Revolution*, and *Sheena and Other Gothic Tales*. He has written numerous nonfiction books, including *Scientific Romance in Britain, 1890-1950*, *Glorious Perversity: The Decline and Fall of Literary Decadence*, and *Science Fact and Science Fiction: An Encyclopedia*. He has contributed hundreds of biographical and critical entries to reference books, including both editions of *The Encyclopedia of Science Fiction* and several editions of the library guide, *Anatomy of Wonder*. He has also translated numerous novels from the French language, including several by the feuilletonist Paul Féval and various classics of French scientific romance.

Lightning Source UK Ltd.
Milton Keynes UK
05 August 2010

157977UK00001B/40/P